The One Homicide Act

Elizabeth Green

AOS Publishing, 2024

Copyright © 2024

Elizabeth Green

All rights reserved under International
and Pan-American copyright conventions

ISBN: 978-1-998662-17-3

Cover Design: Chanelle Poupart

Visit AOS Publishing's website:

www.aospublishing.com

Miami Tribune, May 8, 2023: Governor Swift Signs Controversial "Murder Law"

In yesterday's special election, Florida voters passed the One Homicide Act by a margin of seventy-four percent. Governor Mark Swift released a statement proclaiming the move "a big step forward in the fight against the state's rising tide of violent crime."

The law, which has been protested by victims' rights groups, gun control advocates, and criminal justice reform organizations, allows each Florida resident to commit one murder with no legal consequences. The State House is currently drafting the statutes of the law, due to be ratified in the coming week.

The law was drafted by State Senator David Hume. At a press conference in March, he explained, "Florida's crime rate is skyrocketing. The nation's crime rate is skyrocketing. The One Homicide Act is the result of exhaustive research into law enforcement trends and psychology. If people have a controlled outlet for their aggression, they will be less likely to commit repeated violent crimes. The legal system is too bogged down in bureaucracy to truly help the people. This will give people who have been denied justice a second chance." He stressed that this would not "lead to anarchy," after a reporter raised the concern that "there would be killing and mayhem in the streets." Hume countered, "There will be strict rules governing these homicides. Anyone who violates these rules will be prosecuted to the full extent of the law."

Hume explained his reasoning behind the law. "We have tried so many different tactics, mandatory minimum sentencing, drug crackdowns, juvenile interventions, and yet Florida's violent crime rate remains among the highest in the nation. America's crime rate is the highest in the developed world. We need to take drastic action to change that. I know how it sounds, but I believe it could work. The answer isn't more laws, more government, but less. The people deserve the right to govern themselves."

State and national law enforcement have expressed divided opinions on the measure. Miami Metro Police interim Chief Bernard Wayne and assistant Attorney General Tyrone Reynolds stood behind Governor Swift today when he signed the bill. Reynolds, who initially opposed the law, says he changed his mind after reviewing "several studies."

"It sounds counterintuitive, but I believe this law will decrease crime," he said in a press conference yesterday. "I had a meeting with Governor Swift where he showed me additional studies, and they were compelling. Crime in Florida is on the rise with no end in sight. I'm willing to try anything."

However, the new law also drew the ire of many in the state's law enforcement community. Miami police chief Ray Gonzalez resigned in protest yesterday upon news of the law's passing. "All this does is pave the way for vigilantism," he said in an interview with this reporter. "Vigilantism is the enemy of law and order. This will backfire, I promise you." Chief Gonzalez sent a letter to Governor Swift last week asking him to veto the law, signed by over one hundred high-ranking Florida police officers, as well as the Miami-Dade County prosecutor and two retired judges. Swift's office did not respond to inquiries regarding this letter.

Hume's original draft of the One Homicide Act contained a rider pledging an increase of mental health services in prisons. Majority leader Henry Kane threatened to block voting unless this was removed. It was "too expensive," claimed Kane. Hume agreed to remove the rider, but said he plans to reintroduce the mental health assistance measure in a future session.

The One Homicide Act will go into effect January 1, 2024.

Tampa New Life Church, May 16, 2023: A Message from Reverend Charles Gantry

I have served as Governor Mark Swift's pastor and spiritual advisor for over twenty years. The Bible says an eye for an eye. God smites those who do not obey Him. Christianity, like so much else in our society, has become watered down and weakened by young people who need the world to cater to their fragile sensibilities. The One Homicide Act will act as a deterrent to those who think about doing wrong. They'll know their actions have direct consequences, not just in the next world, but this one.

X, @FLforGunSafety, June 30, 2023

Study after study proves that gun control leads to a decrease in crime. But Swift and Hume would rather let us kill each other before going against the gun lobby. #GunControlNow #Against1HA

X, @backthebadge, July 9, 2023

#1HA encourages disrespect for law enforcement. @flsenatorhume has made anti-police comments and the law doesn't include protection for police. Cop killers should be lined up and shot not given legal protection.

X, @govswift_fl, July 10, 2023

@backthebadge I hear and feel your concerns. I have the utmost respect for the brave officers who risk their lives. I pledge to introduce an amendment to protect them under #1HA

X, @nolawsnomasters, July 22, 2023

#1HA is true freedom. Let the people govern themselves like @flsenatorhume said. Anyways @backthebadge cops already get all their murders for free why shouldn't we? #ACAB

Threads, @miamimarxist91, August 1, 2023

#1HA passed. I declare fat cat hunting season officially open. /thread

So-called 'liberals' ranting against 1HA are capitalists who are too chickenshit to rise up against the oligarchs. They're the ones telling us to vote and not get too angry. Fuck them.

To change the world we need to destroy the old order. And that means taking out some dead weight. Good fuckin riddance #nogoodbillionaires #crushcapitalism /end

2024 Florida Statutes, Title XLVII, Chapter 986

986.01 SHORT TITLE. -- Chapter 986 shall be known and may be cited as the "One Homicide Act."

986.02 LEGISLATIVE INTENT. -- This statute allows every citizen in the state of Florida to commit one homicide in their lifetime, with full immunity from criminal prosecution, pursuant to the rules set forth in this chapter.

986.03 Definitions. – As used in this chapter:

(1) "Legal Homicide" means the one homicide each Florida citizen is permitted to commit pursuant to the rules set forth in this chapter.

(2) "Application" means the Intent to Murder application.

(3) "Murderer" means the person submitting the Intent to Murder application.

(4) "Target" means the person named by the Murderer in the Application.

(5) "Notice" means, depending on context, the Notice of Approval of Legal Homicide, Notice of Rejection of Legal Homicide, or Notice of Target of Legal Homicide.

(6) "Homicide Window" means the time period allotted for the commission of a Legal Homicide, ending at one (1) year after the approval date of the Application.

986.04 General Provisions

(1) Both the Murderer and the Target must be at least 18 years old.

(2) Both the Murderer and the Target must be permanent residents of the State of Florida.

(3) Before commission of a legal homicide, the Murderer must complete the Application pursuant to the guidelines in Section 986.05.

(4) Any citizen with two (2) or more prior second- or third-degree felony convictions or one (1) or more capital, life, or first-degree felony convictions will not be granted a legal homicide.

986.05 Intent to Murder Application

(1) The Application can be submitted either in person at a Florida state government office or online via the Florida.gov website.

(2) The Application must include the following information:

name, birth date, address, and Social Security Number (SSN) of Murderer;

name of Target, birth date and address if known;

Florida state ID of Murderer;

two (2) proofs of residence for Murderer; and

reason for targeting Target, pursuant to Acceptable Motives outlined in 986.06.

(2)(a) Acceptable proofs of residence include; current rental lease, mortgage statement from the prior three (3) months, utility bill, proof of homeowner's or renter's insurance, bank statement, or Florida state tax form no older than three (3) years.

(2)(a)(i) If the Murderer or the Target are found to have a permanent residence outside the State of Florida, the Application will be denied and the Murderer will be charged with fraud pursuant to Section 817.034.

(3) Applications will be reviewed by employees of the State of Florida in the jurisdiction of the Murderer's residence;

(4) The Murderer will receive notification of the Application's approval or rejection within three to five business days.

(4)(a) If the Application is approved, the Murderer will receive a Notice of Approval of Legal Homicide via email and Certified Mail. This Notice will be stamped with a Date of Approval and Homicide Window, ending one (1) year from the Date of Approval. The legal homicide must then be commissioned pursuant to Section 986.07.

(4)(b) If the Application is rejected, the Murderer will receive a Notice of Rejection of Murder via email and Certified Mail. The Notice will include a detailed explanation for the Application's rejection. The Murderer will retain their Legal Homicide.

(4)(b)(1) The Murderer can apply again to kill the same Target no sooner than six (6) months after receiving the Notice. If the second Application to kill that Target is rejected, the Murderer cannot apply to kill that Target again.

(4)(c) If the Murderer kills the Target before the Application is approved, all due legal consequences apply. The Murderer will retain their Legal Homicide, pursuant to the outcome of the judgment and the provisions of Section 986.04(4).

(5) The Target will be notified by a Notice of Target of Legal Homicide via email and United States Post Office Certified Mail. This Notice will include the Murderer's name and the start and end date of the one-year timeframe as outlined in 986.05(3)(a).

(6) If two or more persons want to commit one Legal Homicide on the same Target together, each participant must submit a separate Application, along with the Group Homicide addendum identifying and signed by all intended Murderers. This will constitute the legal homicide for all Murderers named on the Application.

986.06 Accepted Motives for Legal Homicides

(1) The Murderer must prove that the Target engaged in one (1) or more of the practices listed below for a legal homicide to be granted:

Theft of Murderer's property or other assets;

Engaging in fraud or deceit to the detriment of the Murderer;

Causing severe physical harm to the Murderer;

Engaging in criminal harassment of the Murderer; and

Violating a protective order pursuant to Section 714.30.

(1)(a) The Murderer must provide at least two (2) forms of proof of the alleged infraction. Acceptable forms of proof include:

Protective order against the Target;

Deposition transcript;

Arrest report;

Private incident report from a place of business or homeowners association (HOA);

Collection notice of unpaid debt; and

Records of written or verbal threats against the Murderer.

(2) The following motives will not be considered as acceptable for a Legal Homicide:

Divorce;

Romantic rejection; and

Employment rejection or termination.

(2)(a) If the Murderer can prove that any of the above motives led to significant physical or emotional distress, or financial hardship, using evidence pursuant to 986.06(1)(a), the Application will be given further consideration.

(3) Any motive that does not fall into the categories already discussed in this section will be decided on a case-by-case basis.

986.07 Commission of Legal Homicides

(1) The Legal Homicide must be completed within the Homicide Window given on the Notice of Approval.

(1)(a) If the Murderer believes they will not be able to complete the legal homicide within the Homicide Window, they can file an Extension of Murder Application. The Murderer must provide at least one (1) document as proof of a hardship that will prevent the completion of the Legal Homicide in the Homicide Window. The following items are permitted as evidence of hardship:

letter from a medical professional;

hospital record;

court summons; or

record of incarceration.

1(b) The Extension must be filed no later than sixty (60) days before the Homicide Window End Date, as defined in Section 4(a). Any Extension received after that time will be denied.

(1)(c) If the Extension is approved, the Murderer will receive a Notice of Homicide Window Extension via email and Certified Mail with a new Date of Approval and the new Homicide Window. The Extension will extend the Homicide Window for one (1) year after the new Date of Approval.

(1)(d) If the Extension is rejected, the Murderer will have until the end of the initial Homicide Window to carry out the Legal

Homicide. If the Legal Homicide is not carried out, the penalties listed in Section 986.07(2) apply.

(2) If the murderer does not complete the homicide in the Homicide Window or the approved Extension period, the Murderer cannot apply to kill the listed Target again. Both the Murderer and the Target will receive a Notice of Failure to Complete Legal Homicide. The Murderer will retain their Legal Homicide.

(3) If the Murderer kills a person other than the Target identified on the approved Application, all due legal consequences apply.

(3)(a): If that homicide is ruled a non-criminal act under self-defense or Stand Your Ground legislation, the Murderer will still have their legal homicide. If the murder is not found to be self-defense, the Murderer forfeits their legal homicide.

(4) If the Murderer commits their approved homicide of the named Target outside the state of Florida, the Murderer must provide the Notice of Approval of Legal Homicide to the local authorities.

(4)(a) Every Notice of Approval of Legal Homicide will include instructions to out-of-state law enforcement to remand the Murderer to Florida for evaluation of the Legal Homicide.

986.08 Rights of Target

(1) The Target has the right to defend themselves against attacks by the Murderer, but cannot seek protection from law enforcement.

(1)(a) If the Target kills the Murderer during commission of the Murderer's Legal Homicide, it will be considered self-defense and not subject to legal consequences. The Target will retain their Legal Homicide.

986.09 Evaluation of Legal Homicide

(1) After the commission of the Legal Homicide, the Murderer must alert State authorities that the Homicide has occurred via telephone or in person to the police jurisdiction where the Legal Homicide occurred. If the notification is made via telephone, the Murderer must report to the appropriate police precinct within twenty-four (24) hours of the call.

(2) After the notification, the police in the jurisdiction of the Legal Homicide will review the evidence to ensure the Legal Homicide was commissioned in accordance with the statutes in this section.

2(a) If the Legal Homicide is found to be in accordance with the relevant statutes, the Murderer will sign a Notice of Completion of Legal Homicide acknowledging that they have used their one (1) Legal Homicide.

2(b) If the Legal Homicide is not found to be in accordance with the relevant statutes, the police in the jurisdiction of the Legal Homicide must conduct a standard homicide investigation.

2(b)(i) If the Murderer is found legally culpable in an unauthorized Homicide, they will face all due legal consequences. The Murderer will retain their Legal Homicide.

986.10 Special Provisions

(1) Murderers cannot name their children, biological or adopted, as Targets.

(2) Murderers can name their parents as Targets only under special circumstances, such as;

Physical abuse;

Disinheritance; and

Removal of livelihood, i.e. a trust or other financial support, if the Murderer can prove such removal caused significant financial hardship.

(2)(a) Proof of these special circumstances must be provided pursuant to 986.06(1)(a).

American Association of Mental Health Professionals, January 2024 Newsletter: Editorial: The One Homicide Act poses a serious danger to mental health

It is with great disappointment that we at the AAMHP learned of the passing of the One Homicide Act in Florida. The United States already has a poor track record of adequately treating mental health. As a psychiatrist who has been practicing for over twenty years, the last six in the Florida prison system, I can say with reasonable certainty that the One Homicide Act will only make things worse.

First, the law shows a poor understanding of the average motives of homicide. The majority of murders are impulsive, not planned. The one shred of light is that it could force those who want to kill to examine their motives and wait, but I fear they will be in the minority.

Motives for murder are unpredictable and often insignificant, bordering on petty. Many are the result of emotion overtaking logic. Florida State Senator David Hume, who drafted the law, says it is his hope that it will be used to correct imbalances in the justice system, and that the One Homicide Act will not lead Florida into anarchy. Hume's optimism is unrealistic. He does not appear to understand the nuances of criminal motivation. Many applicants will only see a green light to take violent revenge for any perceived slight.

Hume says that "proper precautions will be ensured." I reviewed the statute, and I urge all of my colleagues to do the same. Many of the guidelines for applications are open to interpretation and could easily be abused. What are the parameters for "excessively personal"? The state employees reviewing the applications are as human as the rest of us. How do we know they'll make the right decisions, unblinded by personal biases?

I can also add my experience with the Florida judicial system and the current administration as supporting points in my skepticism of the One Homicide Act. Since his election in 2020, Governor Swift has proven himself a dangerous figure for those struggling with mental health. He vetoed a bill that would provide free counseling for prisoners with substance abuse, on the grounds that it would "cost too much" and "encourage drug use among children," which of course is nonsense. All of this was a smokescreen for Swift's true motive: to keep marginalized populations down and keep the state's for-profit prisons full. Correction Solutions of America, the second largest operator of private prisons in the nation, which has its headquarters in Jacksonville, contributed heavily to Swift's last campaign. He even gave a speech at their end-of-year conference in 2022.

Mark Swift's judgment and actions have proven suspect time and again in matters of criminal justice or mental health. The One Homicide Act is dangerous, and the mental health community must do everything in our power to oppose it.

State Senator David Hume, Official Website, January 5, 2024: Why I introduced the One Homicide Act

I was happy to hear that the voters of Florida passed the One Homicide Act. However, I know other citizens have concerns about their safety and the efficacy of the law.

I want to assure my fellow Floridians that the One Homicide Act will be enforced in good faith and all applications will be thoroughly vetted. I am currently speaking with Governor Swift to increase the budget for training and new employees.

I drafted this law because, as it is, the legal system all too often lets its citizens down. There are too many appeals, chances for criminals to slip through the cracks, and police officers and lawyers serving special interests instead of the people.

The case of Ken McElroy in Missouri was an influence in creating the One Homicide Act. McElroy was a tyrant who terrorized the town of Skidmore through robberies and assaults. Charges after charges were filed against him, but none ever stuck to him. The people were living in fear, with no other options. Then one of the local residents killed him and nobody said anything to the police. This person did the whole town a favor, and they were grateful. They were all better off without McElroy. The One Homicide Act will allow Florida residents to rid themselves of their own Ken McElroys who have evaded traditional justice. Applicants who can prove they were wronged by the courts and the legal system will be given priority.

The One Homicide Act is unprecedented, which unfortunately means there will be bumps in the road. But I believe it will be worth it to make new advances in crime prevention and to increase the freedom of the people.

TikTok, @fl_libertarian73, Ted Howard, February 6, 2024: #1HA is a big step for freedom

"Hey y'all, big news here in Florida, ya probably heard. Anybody here can kill once with no consequence. Awesome. Thank you Governor Swift and David Hume for 1HA. One step closer to total freedom. Freedom for human nature to thrive, uncaged by unfair laws and governed only by survival of the fittest. Hey, y'all worried, like, oh, what if somebody tries to kill me? Maybe don't do things that make people wanna kill you. Don't steal, don't invade private property, don't bother anybody. It's simple. Leave people alone and nobody'll wanna kill you. Don't depend on the government to protect you. Look out for yourselves. Be smart, mind your business, don't step on anybody's toes, and nobody'll wanna kill you. 1HA is a good thing. It's giving power back to the people from the clutches of the nanny state. It'll keep all of us in line and remind us that the only one any of us can depend on is ourselves. And if you don't wanna kill anybody don't. They're not making you. Me, I'm definitely gonna kill somebody. Don't know who yet. I got a long list of idiots that don't deserve to breathe our oxygen and can't wait to take one of them out. I'll keep y'all updated."

Palm Beach Post, February 20, 2024: State House rushes changes to One Homicide Act in emergency session

Within one week of the enactment of the One Homicide Act, state government offices received almost eight hundred Intent to Murder applications. At least ten named Governor Mark Swift as the intended victim, with the most common justification given as passing the "immoral" law. Over twenty applications named State Senator and One Homicide Act architect David Hume as the intended victim. Other legislators who supported the law were also named. "See how much you approve of state-sanctioned murder now," one applicant declared.

These applications were denied, and Swift introduced a new addendum: victims cannot be elected officials, and politically motivated murders will not be approved.

The addendum passed the Senate yesterday with an overwhelming eighty-one percent of the vote. However, Senator Hume voted against it, and made his objections clear on his official Facebook page: "My intent was that all citizens have equal access to this new avenue of justice. Just because we're in a position of power doesn't give us the right to give ourselves special treatment."

Threads, @seminole91, March 1, 2024

I don't know who needs to hear this but Gov Swift is no man of the people. He was a Wall Street dude who retired at 40, moved to Florida and bought his way into office with his daddy's money. #1HA is just another way for him and his rich buddies to increase their influence and y'all are buying his BS. Thank you for coming to my Ted talk.

Tallahassee Observer, March 15, 2024: State House administration staff requests More employees to accommodate influx of 1HA applications

After the passing of the One Homicide Act, which allows each Florida resident to kill one person with no legal consequences, several groups have raised concerns, from mental health professionals to criminal justice reform advocates. Now, state employees are voicing grievances with how the law is impacting their jobs.

Yesterday, a State House administration staffer contacted this reporter via email, requesting to remain anonymous: "1HA has created the need for hundreds more man hours, yet we were told by the governor's office that there was only room in the budget for two more employees, both part-time. That is not enough. We're pulling people from other departments, people who already have work to do. We're already stretched thin and this will only make things worse." An email from a manager at the State House confirmed that they have received requests from staff for new employees to accommodate the influx of work in reviewing and approving One Homicide Act applications.

Governor Swift's press secretary said there are no immediate plans to increase the budget for the State House staff but promised additional resources "very soon." When asked for specifics, he said, "The One Homicide Act is projected to cut administrative waste and red tape, freeing more room in the budget. I predict that within two or three months we can fully staff the State House and other institutions that have been short-staffed."

Each of Governor Swift's quarterly budgets over the past year featured a cut for state administrative staff, at an average of twelve percent.

Keysnews.com, April 23, 2024: Senator Ross criticizes One Homicide Act

State Senator Dorothy Ross, who represents Key West, contacted this reporter to discuss the controversial One Homicide Act, which went into effect at the beginning of the year. "I want my opposition to the One Homicide Act to go on the record to my constituents. This law is nothing but a quick fix, if that. It doesn't address the roots of crime. Most people who break the law do so out of desperation, not some 'animal instinct.' They steal because they need money, they beat up somebody on the street out of frustration, they use drugs to cope with hardships. This desperation is caused by poverty and lack of access to necessary resources. Addressing those issues is the real way to lower crime."

Ross introduced a bill to decriminalize all drugs in the same session that saw the passing of the One Homicide Act, citing sociological studies and similar programs in other countries. Ross says Hume supported the measure, which was confirmed by a review of the session transcript, and that she has always had a "good relationship" with Hume. "We disagree on many issues, but I've always had immense respect for him. I told him this thing would cause serious harm and begged him not to go through with it. He showed me studies, gave examples, but they didn't make sense to me. I tried to explain why I disagreed with his conclusion. To his credit, he listened. I was disappointed when he introduced it in session. I'm very sad to say our professional relationship has suffered as a result. I just don't see him the same way I used to."

The transcripts also confirmed Ross' claim that the vast majority in the legislature "refused to even hear" her drug decriminalization proposal. Governor Swift pledged to veto the bill if it reached his desk and went to the Senate floor to issue the statement: "Drugs lead to crime. That's a simple fact. Drug pushers and addicts need to face maximum consequences for endangering themselves and others. Most of the murders in the state are related to drugs. These people don't deserve free medical care paid for by Florida taxpayers. They need to be locked away where they can't do any more damage."

The Florida Association of Addiction Specialists issued a statement supporting Ross' proposal and criticizing Swift's response: "The only reason drugs are associated with crime is because of the criminalization of drugs. Treatment and education, not incarceration, are the way to prevent drug use and associated crimes."

While maintaining her "disgust" with the One Homicide Act, Ross also says its passing has given her "a sense of hope." She plans to reintroduce her decriminalization bill in the next session. "With Florida considering a different apprpach to the crime problem, as ill-advised as it may be, it's my hope they'll consider another unorthodox measure, one that will do far more to prevent crime than letting people kill each other."

Instagram, @offbeattourist: May 2, 2024

In Saint Augustine right now, and I saw something wild, even for Florida. A murder. Right on the street outside the restaurant. We're eating, and this guy is waiting outside. Looking around, like he was waiting for someone. And he was. A few minutes later we heard a shot. Everybody ran outside to see what happened. This girl was lying dead on the sidewalk. The guy was holding a gun, standing over the body. He was smiling. I didn't get any pictures of the shooting. But I got one of the shooter getting into a cop car. I was freaking out thinking how unhinged it was but then I remembered they have that law that people can kill legally here in some situations. I did not have "Florida legalizes murder" on my 2024 bingo card.

Facebook, Florida Small Business Coalition, May 28, 2024: An Open Letter to Governor Mark Swift

Governor Swift,

You said the One Homicide Act would be good for the state of Florida. It would lead to less crime and less bureaucracy. You failed to consider the effect on those of us who have to clean up the messes. All of the undersigned business owners and managers have barred murders on their premises. We have included two stories below to illustrate why this was necessary.

Carla Perez, manager of the Maritime Hotel in Orlando: "Since 1HA, the Maritime has been the site of five murders. Four were committed in guest rooms, but last week a young woman was shot in the middle of our lobby. The guests were horrified. At least one had to be treated for shock. One of my front desk staff quit because he was afraid he'd see another shooting. We don't want to become known as the Murder Hotel. Any guest who commits a murder will be removed from the premises and be held financially responsible for any damages."

Shawn Washington, owner of the Thirsty Gator Bar in Panama City: "Last month there was a stabbing here. It was horrifying. One of our regulars said she was afraid to come back. In response, our staff has started searching customers for weapons. We know the new law and respect the choices of anybody who wants to take advantage of it in private. But we will no longer permit murders on our premises. It's bad for business."

These are just two of many examples. Now that some murders are legal, violent incidents have increased substantially in businesses such as ours and have left employees and patrons traumatized.

The Florida Small Business Coalition is lobbying for an amendment to the One Homicide Act to prohibit murders in public businesses. Our leaders will speak before the State House on Tuesday. We respect the personal choices of Floridians, but our employees and customers have the right to not see someone die a horrible death while trying to work or relax. We hope you and the State legislature will take the above testimony and the 160 signatures below as evidence of the toll this law has taken on businesses.

Facebook, The Stirner Society of Arizona, June 1, 2024: Support the Individual Justice Act

State Senator Max Roarke introduced the Individual Justice Act in committee last week. Inspired by the success of the One Homicide Act in Florida, the law will allow each Arizona resident to kill one person who they feel deserves it. The people who get killed would be people the state and the world will be better off without anyway. It is a much-needed step in the direction of individual freedom. We will be holding a rally/fundraiser in support of Senator Roarke and to get the Individual Justice Act on the ballot in November.

Arizona needs the Individual Justice Act. The whole country does but most parts of this country are overrun with wussy liberals who need their hands held by government bureaucrats or establishment Republicans who have lost sight of the Constitution's promise of personal governance. Arizona can lead the way and show what the country will be when the people govern themselves and the smartest and most capable are allowed to rise to the top, as is their destiny.

Location: Phoenix City Park (across from the State House)

Time: Sunday, June 9 at 12:00

DisneyWorld.com, June 9, 2024: One Homicide Act Murders Prohibited on Park Premises

Last year, the state of Florida passed the One Homicide Act, allowing each Florida resident to commit one murder within the parameters of the law. However, Walt Disney World will continue to prohibit all acts of violence on our premises, including those sanctioned under the One Homicide Act.

This is a happy place for our guests to relax and enjoy themselves. We don't want anything to disrupt that, even if the act of violence is technically "legal." Disney continues to stand for peace and inclusion.

Florida Department of Justice Official Website, June 14, 2024: Summary of State Crime Statistics

Eight months after the passing of the One Homicide Act, convicted homicides other than the legally sanctioned are down twelve (12) percent. Reports of property crimes such as burglaries decreased by forty-three (43) percent, and domestic violence reports have decreased by 18 percent. Reports of armed robberies, drug-related crimes, and sexual assault have not seen any significant changes.

The report is available in the below link.

Sunshine Pride Official Website, June 20, 2024: 1HA causes spike in murders of trans women

Last year, over one hundred trans women assaulted in the state of Florida. Twenty-eight were murdered. That number has increased since the One Homicide Act went into effect at the beginning of this year. Upsettingly, but unsurprisingly, trans women have become a common target under the new law.

Sunshine Pride made a Freedom of Information Act request to obtain Intent to Murder applications naming trans women as victims, or "targets" in the last six months. Our search brought back thirty-two applications, with "fraud" as the most commonly cited motive: "She lied about being a woman." Sixteen men (and all but two applicants who applied to kill trans women identified as men) cited this motive. Fraud is an approved motive for murder under the law, and State Senator Hume specifically said fraud cases would be given preferential treatment in an interview with the Tallahassee Observer last year. Out of the twenty-nine applications, twenty-three were approved.

Trans women already face an astronomical risk of assault and murder in Florida and all over the world. Now attacks on them are state-approved. 1HA is just another way for people to indulge their prejudices against innocent victims just trying to live their lives.

Crimes against trans people are routinely ignored by law enforcement. David Hume said 1HA is for those who were let down by the system. If that isn't the trans community, I don't know who it could be.

Can we use 1HA to fight back against homophobes and bigots? Maybe. Harassment is an approved motive under the law. And how many in our community are regularly harassed to the point of depression and even suicide? But we urge Florida's LGBTQ+ community not to sink to the bottom of the moral barrel with the rest of the state. We're not saying don't defend yourselves. If someone attacks you, or targets you under 1HA for who you are, you have the right and the duty to fight back. But we don't believe that preemptively killing homophobic aggressors is the right solution.

The biggest problem with 1HA, and Stand Your Ground and open carry and "religious freedom" laws, is that the people who most want to take advantage of it are the ones using it for selfish reasons and to further their prejudices and to make themselves feel big. What we need to progress as a society are understanding and cooperation. Not an endless cycle of aggression and retaliation.

Reddit, r/1HAStories, June 23, 2024: 1HA hack for people outside Florida

I live in North Carolina so I can't use 1HA but I figured out a way to fuck with my bitch ex who goes to FSU. I used a copy of the notice that a target gets, you can download it from a bunch of websites, DM me for links, I made up a fake one and sent it to her with a fake name for the murderer. Got a real official looking envelope to put it in. She posted it on Instagram freaking the fuck out. She was like Why would anyone want to kill me? I don't even know who this person is. Maybe one of the good guys you ditched so you could fuck a pretty boy jock with no brain. It was so funny. Next best thing to killing her.

TampaNeighbors.org, Resident Forum, June 27, 2024: As an Albanian immigrant, I see where 1HA is going and it's scary

I came to the US from Albania twelve years ago. Like many immigrants I was looking for a better life. I've lived in Tampa for seven years. I was against 1HA from the beginning, because it felt way too familiar.

In Albania we have gjakmarrja. The closest English translation is blood feud. It's officially outlawed by the government but criminal organizations still use it and the government usually looks the other way.

Gjakmarrja is when someone does something bad, like kills or beats up someone, the victim's family kills a member of the attacker's family. It can go on for many generations. People who had nothing to do with the original crime end up paying for it. I was listening to my coworker and he said his brother got killed under 1HA so he was going to kill the killer's family "so they know how it feels." This person he wanted to kill did nothing wrong. I just hope his application doesn't get approved. Though who's to say if that will stop him. 1HA has turned Florida into Albania. But worse, because it's approved by the law.

I love Tampa. I love my job, my friends, and the life I built here. I never thought I'd leave but now I feel like I might have to.

Florida, don't become Albania. Repeal 1HA.

Florida.gov, Jobs, June 30, 2024: Application assessors

The Department of Homicide Assessment is seeking dedicated individuals to review Intent to Murder applications submitted under the One Homicide Act.

Job duties:

Receive Intent to Murder applications through the Florida.gov online portal

Review applications in accordance with legal and standard practices

Send approval or rejection notices to applicants

Send notifications to selected targets for approved applications

Maintain records of approved and rejected applications

Required qualifications:

Must be able to pass a Florida state government employee background check

At least two (2) years of experience in a government or private administrative position

Proficient in e-filing and database processes

Instagram: @pensacola_nurse84, July 2, 2024, Location: Pensacola General Hospital

Everybody in Florida's talking about 1HA but nobody's talking about the drain it's creating on our healthcare system. I've been working in emergency medicine for seven years now and it's always been bad but never like this. Before it was what you'd expect, car crashes, accidents, dumb drunk people, ODs, domestic violence victims. We still have all of that but now it also seems like at least three times a week we see someone who just barely escaped getting killed under 1HA. We had a 19-year-old girl tonight who got stabbed by her ex-boyfriend. Knife missed her heart by just a couple inches. She almost bled out. She's only alive because she managed to run out of her house and flag down a car that took her to the hospital. And because of 1HA the guy's gonna get away with it. I didn't vote for 1HA but I didn't think it would be this bad. I never thought so many people would wanna kill. And it's only gonna get worse. #Repeal1HA

TikTok, @miamimogul72: Achievement Unlocked, #1HA kill

Hey y'all, I did it. I killed somebody under 1HA. And it felt fucking great. The target was this asshole inspector holding up construction on my new development. Said there were safety violations. The place was fine. My company's inspector signed off on it. This guy just had it out for us.

I followed him home and as he got out of his car I came up behind him and stabbed him. Blood was everywhere. I got to watch that piece of shit die. He was costing me and my employees money and holding up construction on the homes of people who need them. I'm not fucking sorry. One less bureaucrat, the world's better off.

The 1HA rule against killing politicians doesn't apply to government employees. I checked with my lawyer. If you hate the government there is a way to get back at them.

After it was over I called the cops, showed them the body and my approval notice, they took me to the station and I had to fill out some paperwork and show my ID and that my murder was completed. I was out in less than 20 minutes.

1HA is the best thing that ever happened to Florida. It's so much easier than going through the courts and bureaucratic knots. None of them will tell me how to run my company ever again.

KeysNews.net, July 20, 2024: Measure Banning One Homicide Act Murders in City Limits Passes

According to a Gallup poll from last month, seventy-one percent of Florida residents support the One Homicide Act, but Key West does not. Eighty-seven percent of residents voted against it in last year's special election, and the district's Senator, Dorothy Ross, is one of the law's most outspoken opponents in the state legislature. Yesterday, the city council voted to ban any One Homicide Act murders in the city limits.

"This will be a safe space in Florida," Mayor Paula Torres said in a press conference. "Key West has a reputation as a place for relaxation. People come here for our beautiful beaches, wildlife, and easygoing environment. Our residents and visitors can't relax if they think they'll be targeted for murder. Or if they think they'll turn the corner and see somebody getting shot. Which is happening all over the state because of the One Homicide Act. It may be the law, but that doesn't mean we can't take precautions to respect the wishes of our residents. Yes, Floridians now have the right to kill. But they can't do it in our town."

Threads, @beachtownmillennial, July 24, 2024

My friend got killed yesterday under 1HA. It's one of those things you never think will happen to you. It's so frustrating that my friend got murdered and that's just it. Cause it's legal. 1/

I voted in favor of 1HA. I thought it would be for DV or SA victims to take out their attackers. Or a way for those of us on the bottom to level the playing field against the billionaires. But I guess that's not what's happening. 2/

I don't even know the guy who killed her. He said she broke into his house. I admit she's had problems with drugs but that seems drastic. What is the screening process? Did he even try filing charges before he jumped to murder? And what if he lied? Do they check for that? 3/

My friend wasn't perfect. She had a lot of problems. But she didn't deserve to die. #Repeal1HA /end

Sarasota Martial Arts Academy Official Website, July 30, 2024: Special Offer for 1HA Targets

If you've been targeted under the One Homicide Act, I can help give you an edge.

As an FBI agent, I learned how to defend myself against the worst of the worst. Ever since 1HA a lot of people have been coming in trying to learn self-defense skills. After hearing this, I created classes specifically to teach countermeasures to the most common murder methods.

I teach how to listen for intruders, the best ways to take cover, how to fall to minimize injury. Everything I teach I learned in the FBI academy or on the job.

Show your 1HA Target Notification and get 15 percent off

your first class.

Miami Tribune, August 2, 2024: Retired detective, advocacy groups question efficacy of One Homicide Act

John Kramer, a former Miami Metro homicide detective, gave an interview to this publication to share his opinion of the One Homicide Act.

"I don't believe this will lead to a decrease in homicide in the long run. Most murders are committed in a flash of extreme emotion. They're committed in the heat of the moment, not planned.

Allowing citizens to apply to commit murders will not change that."

The state chapter of the Gun Control Alliance also condemned 1HA in a statement on the group's website: "This law will not help the woman being accosted by her abusive husband and his legally obtained firearm. It won't help the victims of the many mass shootings in this country. If you want to prevent murder, keep the tools for murder away from dangerous people."

An attorney with the Florida chapter of the Citizens for Criminal Justice Reform agreed. "Why do we always try to solve our violence problem with more violence? Governor Swift and his Republican senate have repeatedly cut programs to help the poor. Why aren't we investing in health care and programs to alleviate poverty? That's how you fight crime. Attack it at its source."

A representative of Women of the Sunshine State, a women's rights advocacy group, contacted this reporter to "go on record saying 1HA is bad for women. I voted for it because I thought it would give women an equal shot against a sexist system. But we've heard reports from women saying their applications to kill their abusers who ignore restraining orders and harass them are being denied. Yet men applying to kill women are overwhelmingly approved for absurd reasons. Governor Swift's administration has never been good for women, and 1HA is making it worse."

Governor Swift's office did not respond to requests for comment.

WTF.com, August 4, 2024: "She scratched my car when pulling out of the parking lot": 10 of the Wildest Motives for Murder From Florida One Homicide Act Applications

Last year Florida out-Florida-ed itself with the One Homicide Act, or 1HA. Now anybody there can kill one person and totally get away with it no questions asked as long as they fill out an application. So yeah, basically an entire state woke up and literally chose violence. Florida state employees who review "Intent to Murder" applications (how are those a real thing?) recently took to Reddit to share some of the most unhinged motives for (legal) murder they've seen.

1. "Someone stole an orchid from his greenhouse. That's it. A. F---ING ORCHID. And guess what? Application approved. The system is broken."

2. "A girl wouldn't go on a second date with him. Toxic masculinity at its finest. At least it got rejected."

3. "Her neighbor chopped down a tree, and some branches fell into her yard. The branches caused damage to her garden and decreased the property value. I rejected it but got overruled by my supervisor. I quit a week later. 0/10 recommend working for the Florida govt right now."

4. "He went on a date with a girl who he later learned was transgender. He said it was fraud. And it got approved. Transphobia, cool motive in 2024. But what do you expect from the home of Don't Say Gay?"

5. "Her co-worker spread rumors about her that cost her a promotion. It sucks but maybe talk to HR? People get passed over every day and manage not to go full supervillain. I didn't get that one but my idiot coworker approved it. Don't know how much longer I'll last here."

6. "She said a man was trying to kidnap her son. Because he was 'always looking at him' on the playground. Maybe the guy was there with his kid? Men can be parents too. Update your gender stereotypes. Definitely rejected that one. Seriously Florida and humanity, do better."

7. "His ex-wife got more alimony out of him. He said it was under false pretenses and wanted to kill her. Who wants to bet there's more to this story? Why didn't he go after the judge who awarded the alimony? I know, because he just hated his ex. Application approved because Florida and the rest of the world hates women."

8. "He said a mover stole a gun from his collection. Police said the mover didn't do it, but the guy wouldn't let it go. Said it had to be him. It was rejected, which, I guess, a little faith in humanity restored."

9. "He got kicked out of a bar for starting a fight. He applied to kill the person he fought with for 'ruining his reputation in the community.' I think you did that yourself buddy. It got rejected. Good thing too, cause I woulda had to fling myself off the planet if that one got approved."

10. "A dude wanted to kill his brother-in-law for spending too much time with his (the applicant's) son. The brother-in-law was gay and the applicant thought it was 'grooming.' It was approved. Florida homophobia in full force. Quit the next day. Now trying to move out of Florida."

Miami Metro News, August 11, 2024: Murder of podcast host ignites 1HA debate in right-wing community

Jesse Tucker, conservative commentator and host of the Trigger Happy podcast, was shot and killed two weeks ago outside his West Palm Beach home. The perpetrator, Tucker's former employee Mary Kellerman, was determined to have acted lawfully under the One Homicide Act. Tucker was the first high-profile victim, or target, killed under the controversial law passed in last year's special election.

Tucker, a prominent figure in conservative media, was an outspoken supporter of the One Homicide Act, or 1HA. He interviewed State Senator David Hume in the week before the vote, where he said, "Thank you for the One Homicide Act. I hope it catches on in the rest of the country." Tucker devoted significant time leading up to last year's special election imploring his listeners to vote for the law. "It will be good for the state of Florida, and for the country," he said in one episode. "We've gotten too soft relying on government bureaucrats to solve our problems. We need to go back to our roots, before appeals and public defenders and due process. Solve our problems man to man. Vote 1HA."

Despite accusations of political motives, Mary Kellerman's stated motive, both in her application and in her mandated post-murder interview at the police station, never cited politics. She said she killed Tucker because he fired her after she rejected his sexual advances. "Then," she said, "he spread lies about me that made it almost impossible to find another job. He also went weeks without paying me, and didn't pay me at all for the last month I was there." Deception and imposing financial hardship are listed as acceptable motives for murder under 1HA.

Kellerman came forward with allegations against Tucker after her firing last year, in an interview with the online publication Florida Independent, but Tucker denied the charges. He dismissed Kellerman as "a disgruntled former employee," on his show and on X, and insinuated that she attempted to seduce him to further her career.

Tucker's supporters have drafted an online petition calling for Kellerman to be charged with fraud in her application. "Any woman now can say a man touched her and everybody believes it," a comment from one signatory reads. "Jesse Tucker was an American hero and his legacy can't be tarnished by a lying [expletive]."

A spokesperson for Governor Mark Swift, who appeared on Tucker's podcast shortly after the passing of the One Homicide Act, responded to Tucker's murder on X: "The Governor was deeply saddened to hear about the death of Jesse Tucker, a man he considered a friend. The office of the Governor still believes in the

One Homicide Act and promises to review Ms. Kellerman's application in light of allegations of fraud."

State Senator David Hume wrote in response to an email requesting comment: "A member of my staff reviewed Ms. Kellerman's application and found it to be in full compliance with the terms of the One Homicide Act. I have shared this information with the Governor."

Mary Kellerman and her attorney did not respond to our emails.

Representative Claudia Santiago Official Website, August 16, 2024: Video: Claudia Santiago Accepting the Nomination as Democratic Candidate for Governor

Almost every voter and reporter has asked for my opinion on the One Homicide Act. It's sad that this is what the nation sees when they think of Florida. As a delegate, I voted against it. As Governor, I will end this destructive law that has made Florida a national laughingstock. But more than that, it's ruining our state's morale. It's ruining our economy. Please read the study linked below. Over nine thousand residents have left Florida since the passing of 1HA. If elected, I will do everything in my power to get rid of the One Homicide Act and make Florida a safe and prosperous place for all of its citizens once again.

Orlando Sentinel, August 17, 2024: Fort Myers Teens Charged with Distributing Fake 1HA Target Notifications

A group of high school students in Fort Myers were arrested after sending forged Target Notifications, which alert people named as Targets under the One Homicide Act. The scheme was uncovered after Lenora Waters, a teacher at the offenders' school, Fort Meyers South High, received a notice. "I read it and I had never heard of the person who supposedly wanted to kill me. It said I totaled his car in an accident last month. I don't drive. I don't own a car. I ride my bike to work. I went to City Hall and showed it to them. They said it was on the wrong kind of paper. I told the story to another teacher, and she said the same thing happened to her. That was when we alerted the police."

The offenders, sixteen-year-old Pablo Gomez, eighteen-year-old Kevin Dryden, and seventeen-year-old Tim Campbell, claimed to have gotten the idea for the fake target notices from Reddit. The user behind the initial post, under the username Morpheus_Durden, was identified as eighteen-year-old Bill Andrews when he was apprehended two weeks ago at his home in Durham, North Carolina, for falsifying government documents. Andrews is currently awaiting trial.

Charges for Gomez, Dryden, and Campbell will be determined after further investigation, a spokesperson for the Fort Myers police department said in a statement.

Florida Independent, August 21, 2024: City clerk questions new crime statistics following the One Homicide Act

The official crime statistics released on Florida.gov yesterday, the first such information released since the passage of the One Homicide Act, indicate a general decline in violent crime. State Senate president David Hume, the law's architect, and Miami Metro Police Chief Bernard Wayne touted these findings in a press conference. "This was a bold experiment, with a very real chance for failure," Hume's opening statement began, "but the crime numbers speak for themselves." Wayne, who initially opposed the law, added that he has heard from officials in other states interested in passing similar laws.

However, a former Gainesville city clerk speaking under the condition of anonymity raised questions about the crime rates, specifically pointing to the decline in reported robberies. She claims to have reviewed over four hundred Intent to Murder applications and revealed the most common motive: the intended victim stole from the murderer.

The former clerk says she presented her findings to a representative for the city police, posing the question: Are burglaries really decreasing, or are people using the One Homicide Act to take the law into their own hands? She theorized that, rather than decreasing, burglaries were simply no longer being reported, since the law "lets people take revenge on thieves." An attack on property is listed as a justifiable reason to approve an Intent to Murder application. She claims that the police rep dismissed her concerns as "immaterial." The anonymous clerk also claims to have heard an officer say about the One Homicide Act, "Less work for us."

The clerk says she was fired for raising objections to the application review process. "They said I was approving 'frivolous' applications. I didn't consider a woman who applied to murder her ex-boyfriend who was stalking her and terrorizing her frivolous. It wasn't excessively personal. This woman feared for her life and official channels did nothing for her. If anyone needed 1HA, it was her. But I think it was because I approved an application for a woman who applied to kill the neighborhood watch chairperson who shot her son. The watchman was protected under Stand Your Ground. The woman disagreed. I thought she had a good reason so I approved it. But my boss overruled me and rejected it. The next day I was fired. I did some Googling and found out that the watchman was a buddy of Swift." The source provided the name of the intended victim, and campaign finance records revealed him to be a prominent Orlando business owner who contributed over one hundred thousand dollars to Swift's reelection campaign.

The clerk says she emailed her concerns to Swift's office and the state police headquarters, and received almost identical form letters from both, citing the positive effect of the law on the state's crime rates. "They were basically the same," she says. "They said they appreciated my concern but they were happy with the outcome of the new law."

Governor Swift and the police union did not respond to requests for comment.

Threads, @recoveringcop: August 28, 2024

I left the force two years ago but I still know people in Miami Metro. I asked a friend about Bernard Wayne. He was Deputy Chief when #1HA first made the news. He was against it but then after the vote he suddenly supported it. It was weird. /thread

My friend said that there were rumors that Gov Swift promised to use his influence to make Wayne Chief if he supported 1HA. Chief Gonzalez made an announcement before the vote that he would resign if it passed.

Disclaimer that I have no evidence to support this claim. But my friends in Miami Metro all think it's possible. Wayne was always a dick so I kinda believe it.

I'm still on the fence re 1HA. It could be a good thing if it actually helped people who got screwed over by the police and the legal system. But as it is under Gov Swift it's just a tool for vigilantism. Like Chief Gonzalez said.

1HA should definitely be repealed at least until all the problems get sorted out. As it stands there's just too much potential for abuse. /end

Florida for Governor Swift campaign ad: Don't Kill 1HA

The One Homicide Act has led to a decrease in crime and has a seventy percent approval rating among the people of Florida. Governor Mark Swift will uphold this revolutionary stand for individual rights. Claudia Santiago will destroy it.

While serving in the State legislature, Claudia Santiago voted against Stand Your Ground and the One Homicide Act. As governor, she will take away your right to defend yourself and turn justice over to government bureaucrats. She wants to turn us into victims. Defend your rights. Vote Mark Swift.

I'm Mark Swift, and I approve this message.

**Tampa Free Press, September 8, 2024: "Murder tourists"
lead to another round of debate on the One Homicide Act**

According to sources at the State House, State Senator Yolanda Rosenblum is planning to introduce a new amendment to the controversial One Homicide Act that would require applicants to provide two proofs of residency and a Florida tax return for the previous year. The measure is expected to pass.

A spokesperson for Rosenblum's office told this reporter that the amendment was inspired by the influx of what have become known as "murder tourists": out of state visitors coming to Florida for the sole purpose of taking advantage of the One Homicide Act. Police and courts say they have encountered over one hundred such instances since the law passed. One such tourist was a

Tennessee man who listed his friend's address on his application to kill his ex-wife, who lived outside Orlando. There are also allegations of residents "renting out" their Florida addresses to non-residents so they can file 1HA applications. The attorney general's office say they are currently investigating these claims.

"Who knows how many other loopholes there are?" State Senator Dorothy Ross, 1HA's most vocal critic in the State House, said in a press conference. "How can a law that has literal life and death consequences be so poorly drafted? I opposed it then, and I oppose it now. But if it has to stay on the books, it needs to be tighter and less open to abuse."

State Senator David Hume, creator of 1HA, addressed the proposed amendments in a statement at his office: "I still believe in the One Homicide Act, and still believe that the people deserve as much freedom as possible in its execution. However, due to some bad actors, it appears that some restrictions are needed. I will review the amendments and ensure that the basic freedom and my intent for 1HA are preserved."

The vote on the new amendment is scheduled to take place later this week.

Miami Underground, September 30, 2024: Former county employee fears "chain reaction of murder" due to 1HA

Gloria Rodriguez, former clerk manager at the Miami-Dade County Courthouse, is the latest state employee to voice concerns about the One Homicide Act. "The killings will just trigger further killings, further animosity, a further sense of unease. It will create a chain reaction of murder," she wrote in an email to this publication. She says she tried to take the story to the Miami Tribune, but "they never wrote back."

In particular, Rodriguez says she was deeply troubled by the story of Gina Domingo. Domingo's husband Raul was killed four months after 1HA went into effect. Domingo then applied to kill her husband's killer, Herbert Young, citing "severe emotional trauma" and "loss of family income," since the couple had three children. Her application was approved, and Domingo completed the murder of Young earlier this year. "What happens if one of Herbert Young's family members applies to kill Gina for the same reason? Where will it end?" Rodriguez said in an interview with this reporter.

A current county employee interviewed under the condition of anonymity shares Rodriguez's worry: "I don't even work in that department, but they had to bring in extra people to review all the applications coming in, and I got moved over there. In the last few days, I've read a lot that were getting back at other people for killing someone they knew under 1HA. I approved them because you know, they deserve some justice. But yeah, it will probably keep going like that."

Rodriguez says she tried to raise her concerns with her manager at the State House, but "he didn't wanna hear it." She also says she sent emails to Governor Swift but did not receive a response. "When I tried to schedule a meeting with him," she says, "his assistant hung up on me." She also called State Senator David Hume, architect of 1HA, but "his office never called me back."

A staffer in State Senator Hume's office wrote in response to an email from this reporter: "Senator Hume, while remaining mindful of the concerns of abuse, still believes in 1HA. He is continually revisiting it and revising it in response to these concerns."

Governor Swift did not respond to requests for comment.

One-Stop News Source, October 3, 2024: Livestream murders cast harsh light on Florida "murder law"

Shortly after the passing of Florida's controversial One Homicide Act, which allows each resident of the state to commit one murder with no legal consequences, videos of murders started popping up on social media. Reddit is a hotbed of such content, in subreddits like "1HA Stories."

"Can you believe this is legal?" one Redditor wrote, later detailing how he killed his "lying bitch ex." The post's comments were supportive: "Bitch had it coming,"; "I'm f---ing moving to Florida," and, "The hardest part'll be choosing just one person to kill."

The thread also features tips on how to obtain or fake Florida citizenship to take advantage of the law. One Redditor posted their neighbor's address with the comment: "Use it, any of you. This prick is a POS. The only reason I haven't killed him yet is I'm not 18."

The page also features videos taken as users stab, shoot, and strangle their victims. Similar videos have been shared on Facebook, Twitter, and TikTok. One particularly graphic video, which originated on TikTok, went viral across different platforms. It featured a young man, initially known only by the username @panhandledude22 but whose real name was quickly revealed through his other social media accounts as Tony Hardin of Ocala, stabbing a young woman through the neck. "I can't believe I'm gonna get away with this. God bless America." The caption for the video included the hashtag #GettingAwayWithMurder. The video was quickly taken down from Facebook and YouTube, but remains on Reddit and TikTok.

The outrage caused by these videos has triggered a call to repeal the law. Evolved, an anti-1HA group based in Palm Springs, released a statement, "How can any thinking, feeling person possibly support 1HA after seeing this?"

The office of Florida Governor Mark Swift responded to an email inquiry with, "Governor Swift believes that these stories are simply attention seeking from a narcissistic generation. It reflects on them and their ethical failings, not the law. Crime is down. The law is working."

Miami Latinx Voice, October 10, 2024: One Homicide Act amendment would require proof of U.S. citizenship

At a press conference today, Governor Mark Swift announced a pledge to introduce an amendment to the One Homicide Act, which allows each Florida citizen to commit one murder with no legal consequences. Swift's proposal will require the applicant to provide proof of U.S. citizenship.

"There are too many bad people taking advantage of the law in a country where they are not legal residents," Swift said in a press conference.

State Senator and 1HA architect David Hume, according to inside sources, does not support this provision, calling it "unnecessary." Hume posted on X: "The application already requires a Social Security number. That should be enough. Governor Swift and the supporters have not indicated what form this proof of citizenship will take. The whole point of 1HA was to have less bureaucratic red tape in fighting crime, and for everyone to be equal. This will have the opposite effect."

Considering Swift's long history of discrimination and racism against Latinx immigrants, chronicled at length by this publication, the Latinx community in Florida feels this amendment is targeting them. "It's no coincidence that a Latino man just killed the rich white man he worked for who was taking advantage of him, and now there's an amendment that will overwhelmingly impact our community," the spokesperson for the Miami chapter of Unidos US wrote in an editorial on the group's website.

Esteban Torres, the Miami man whose 1HA-approved murder is said to have triggered the new provision, is in fact a U.S. citizen. "Born and raised in Miami, just like my Mama," he said proudly in an interview with this reporter. Earlier this month, Torres, a landscaper, killed his employer, claiming months of unpaid wages. "He refused to pay me and told lies about me after I quit so I couldn't get another job. I tried suing but I couldn't afford the legal fees. I was mad and couldn't see any other way."

Many in Florida's Latinx community applauded Torres' actions and expressed similar plans online. "Maybe I can get that racist prick who forced me out of his neighborhood," read one comment on this publication's initial story about Torres. A FOIA examination of Intent to Murder applications immediately following the Torres story revealed a spike in applications submitted by Latinos, many applying to kill white victims. Though it should be noted that these applications still only accounted for approximately fifteen percent of over two hundred submitted that week.

David Hume Official Website, October 11, 2024: I oppose "citizenship check" for 1HA

I was asked to review Esteban Torres' application by a colleague who claimed that Torres was racially motivated and therefore should have been denied. After my review, I came to a different conclusion. Torres' application followed all the rules and should have been approved.

Governor Swift's citizenship test will only clog the system and create further division among citizens. I also opposed the ban on applications targeting public figures. We're all equal under this law. As public officials, we have security. We're better able to defend ourselves than an ordinary citizen. Giving us extra protection under the law is unnecessary and unfair to other Florida residents, as is requiring a citizenship test. Governor Swift has given no indication of what this test would entail. The lack of transparency on his part in this matter is another reason I find it suspect and pledge to oppose it.

Palm Beach Post, October 28, 2024: Hate crimes provision to 1HA passes

Yesterday, State Senator David Hume announced his proposed "hate crimes" amendment to the One Homicide Act on his official website: "If an application includes any prejudiced slurs or language, it should be instantly rejected. All are equal under the law, and a provision for hate crimes is necessary to preserve equality." Today, the amendment passed the State Senate with just fifty-two percent of the vote.

Governor Mark Swift, who signed the new amendment, could not be reached for comment. However, an anonymous source suggested that Swift did not want to sign it, but was "giving into political pressure."

Reddit, r/FloridiansAgainst1HA: Introduction

Contrary to what you might believe from the news, not everybody in Florida is rushing out to kill because of 1HA. Most of us have no intention of killing anybody. Florida is a beautiful place, not some lawless Mad Max wasteland. There are good people here and a lot of us are against 1HA.

I started this group because of what happened to my neighbor here in Jacksonville. He was 19, skinny scrawny kid. Got killed under 1HA by a dude who was 27, six-six and 250 pounds, all muscle. How was this kid supposed to defend himself against that? It was over something really dumb too. The kid pulled out of his driveway too fast and ran him off the road, damaging his car. Link here: www.jacksonvillebugle.com/neighborhoodnews/1hakilling

I didn't have much of an opinion on 1HA before that happened. I knew I wouldn't be killing anybody but that was about it. Now I want to do everything I can to fight against it. It's just wrong.

EDIT: To all you gun nuts saying if the victim had a gun he would've been fine. He did have a gun. Well his dad did. He couldn't get to it because the killer, who was a lot bigger and stronger, dropped him with one punch right in his doorway and stepped on his chest to keep him from moving before stabbing him. How was he supposed to get to his dad's gun in the other room? Get out of here with your ammosexual propaganda.

To people asking how this guy's application got approved with such a dumb motive, I have the same question. I don't know who's reviewing the applications but they're not doing their job. Another reason 1HA needs to go away.

**Florida Bar Association Newsletter, November 2, 2024:
Circuit court rules that civil suits cannot be filed in response
to One Homicide Act**

In a precedent-setting move, the Palm Beach County Circuit Court has ruled that wrongful death suits cannot be filed in response to the One Homicide Act. In the deciding case, Harris v. Florida, plaintiff Kevin Harris filed a wrongful death suit on behalf of his wife, who was murdered by her ex-husband under the law, claiming that the state erred in approving the murderer's application. Harris' attorney stated that the murderer's application shouldn't have been approved: "In the year before they divorced, the victim filed a domestic violence complaint against her ex-husband. His application should have been more thoroughly vetted. His claim of 'fraud' on the part of the victim was not supported by any substantial evidence." However, the Court sided with the state, saying that the ex-husband's fraud claim was "proven sound." Harris' attorney stated in an interview that he plans to appeal the ruling.

**Arizona.gov, Office of the Governor, November 5, 2024:
Video: Official statement on Individual Justice Act**

Good afternoon. As you know, yesterday, the state of Arizona passed the Individual Justice Act. We were happy to see this historic measure pass by such a large margin of seventy-nine percent. Despite the overwhelming majority of residents supporting this legislation, I would like to take this time to address a few concerns that have been raised since yesterday online and in calls to the state house.

First, yes, the Individual Justice Act was inspired by the success of Florida's One Homicide Act. In the year since that law was passed, Florida has seen a remarkable decrease in crime, a streamlined court, and a boost to its economy. We hope to replicate this success in Arizona, while correcting some of the more troubling aspects of Florida's law.

First and foremost, every citizen will be equal under the Individual Justice Act. Nobody, not even politicians, are exempt from becoming targets. Government should be accountable to its citizens, and this law is no exception. However, we have included a provision protecting our police officers. The whole point of this law is to fight crime, and the police are the first line of defense against crime.

Every application will be given careful consideration. The Arizona State House has hired twenty new employees specifically to review Individual Justice Act applications, in addition to existing employees who have been moved to the newly formed IJA Enforcement Department. In two months, after review of IJA application numbers, the department will conduct a review and, if necessary, hire more personnel. We were well aware of reports from Florida that applications were improperly vetted due to staffing shortages, and we hope to avoid those errors.

Women of the Sunshine State, Official Facebook Page, November 18, 2024: Women treated unfairly in 1HA application process

Much to our disappointment, Governor Mark Swift was re-elected, and his pet project the One Homicide Act is still in full force. 1HA is bad for Florida, in particular its women.

We obtained sixty-five applications of women in Florida who applied to kill men who sexually assaulted them, who were either never brought to trial or, if charged, got acquitted. Over half were rejected. It should be noted that, of fifty-eight rejected applications, forty-two were from women of color. Six of the seven accepted applications were from white women.

State Senator David Hume, who created the law, says the application process is color blind, but women with Spanish last names were overwhelmingly rejected, as were all but one of twelve African-American applicants. The application requires a Social Security number and other identifying information (as it should, we aren't arguing against that per se), which almost certainly leads to identifying an applicant's race.

Hume continues to claim that the One Homicide Act was intended to protect Floridians who were let down by the system, who saw criminals slip through the cracks. Now those women whose abusers got away with it in a court of law are slipping through the cracks again.

First Baptist Church of Atlanta, Official Website, November 27, 2024: A Message from Pastor Adams: Eye for an Eye defeated, thanks to you

I was happy to see the Eye for an Eye Act defeated by Georgia voters. I believe we at First Baptist were integral in the defeat of this immoral law.

Yes, the Bible says an eye for an eye. But the Ten Commandments say "Thou shalt not kill." And Jesus said "Turn the other cheek". The Jesus I believe in helped and healed others. The Jesus I believe in would never want us to solve our problems with murder. The Eye for an Eye Act was nothing but an appeal to the basest instincts of man, the instincts we need to rise above to find a place in the Kingdom of Heaven.

I wanted to do everything in my power to defeat this cruel law. My deacons and I called a meeting of religious leaders from around the state to organize the effort. We had all Christian denominations, Baptist, Methodist, Pentecostal, Presbyterian, Catholic. We had Jews and Muslims. We also had people who didn't identify with any religion who just wanted to support our cause. Hundreds of people from all kinds of backgrounds, races, creeds, and faiths all came together as one. It was truly inspiring. And we did it. We defeated this immoral law. I am so proud of the people of Georgia. And all of you should be proud of yourselves. When we work together, instead of breaking apart along color and religious lines, we can do great things. We can change the world.

State of the Union.org, A Non-Partisan News Review, November 30, 2024: Progressive group urges Florida members to use 1HA to "take out fascists"

Blacklisted, who describe themselves as a "progressive socialist collective", urged their Florida members to use the One Homicide Act as a "tool for revolution." A video on their TikTok account featured their proclaimed "representative", using the name Karkarov, saying, with their face hidden and an apparently modified voice, "This law, passed by Florida's capitalist fascist regime to solidify their police state, can be used against them. The alt-right can't claim moral superiority on this one. It was a Republican governor and a majority Republican legislature who passed it. We're just using it against them, against people who deserve it."

Both the Florida Democratic Party and Green Party denounced Blacklisted's statement. "We are very much opposed to 1HA. We urged Senator Hume from the beginning not to move forward with this dangerous proposition," a spokesperson for the Democratic Party wrote in an email.

In a statement on their website, the Florida Green Party wrote, "Blacklisted does not represent the Green Party platform. Killing people will not solve the crime problems in the state and throughout the country. We believe in implementing change through sound policy and compassion, not violence."

Progressive Florida, a self-described "proud radical leftist movement", also voiced opposition to Blacklisted on Bluesky:

"@blacklisted are going about it all wrong. Progress is made through solidarity not murder. We opposed #1HA from the beginning and oppose it now."

Email inquiries via Blacklisted's official website did not receive a response.

Facebook, Florida Patriot Network, December 1, 2024:
Antifa taking advantage of 1HA to wage culture war

The One Homicide Act was passed to protect law-abiding citizens screwed over by the liberal catch and release justice system. Now Antifa is abusing it in their culture war. Blacklisted, a group that calls fallen soldiers murderers and blocks traffic protesting every time a thug is rightfully shot by the police, is calling on its cult members to "take out the rich." These shiftless losers who don't want to work think they can solve their problems by killing successful job creators, the people who actually work for a living and contribute to society. Sure the liberals whine to take away freedoms from responsible gun owners but when they can kill anybody who doesn't buckle under their commie agenda they suddenly love killing. Libtard hypocrites only care about freedom if it hurts us real Americans.

New York Times, December 9, 2024: Former employee claims Waterson abused Florida's "murder law" to kill enemies

Miami, Fl: According to the former chauffeur of Miami businessman Harry Waterson, currently awaiting indictment for several murders, he and other employees were asked to file Intent to Murder applications under Florida's controversial One Homicide Act (known colloquially as 1HA) to kill enemies of Mr. Waterson. The chauffeur claims that Mr. Waterson, CEO of Palmetto Construction Group, fired him when he refused.

The former employee is asking Florida officials to charge Mr. Waterson with the murder of eight people. He provided pay stubs and contracts given to himself and other employees where Mr. Waterson explicitly stated the name of the victim, or "target", assigned to each employee, and the amount later paid. His attorney claims that Mr. Waterson, in paying employees to file Intent to Murder applications on his behalf, can be charged for murder for hire. He and six of Mr. Waterson's employees are also seeking to have their one legal homicide reinstated.

A search of state records revealed that Harry Waterson used his 1HA murder shortly after the law passed to kill a former business partner who was suing him for breach of contract. Antonio Falco was found strangled in his home, with a note on the body, "Got you now thieving bastard." An investigation revealed that Waterson cited "financial hardship" and "slander" as his motives in the application.

The Miami-Dade County district attorney's office released a statement: "The allegations against Mr. Waterson are currently under investigation. We cannot reveal anything further at this time."

Pro-Choice America, Florida Chapter Official Website, January 30, 2025: Statement on 1HA and its implications for reproductive rights

The One Homicide Act has handed anti-choice extremists a legal loophole to murder abortion providers and supporters. In the four months since the law was enacted, nine doctors have been murdered, with their killers facing no legal consequences, just for doing their jobs. Crusade for the Children explicitly instructed its members to take advantage of the One Homicide Act for this purpose. "I can think of no better use for 1HA than this," the founder said in a statement on their website and on Twitter. In addition, at least four women were murdered by their significant others or families because they got abortions.

Governor Mark Swift has made his hostility toward women's reproductive rights very clear. He voiced support for the highly restrictive Heartbeat Bill, which would ban abortions after the sixth week of pregnancy, before most women even know they're pregnant. We have reached out to State Senator David Hume, who has been a reliable supporter of a woman's right to choose throughout his time in office and has voted against several anti-choice laws. We hope he will listen to us and close this loophole in the law that threatens the already precarious status of reproductive rights in Florida.

@chavez211, TikTok, February 21, 2025: Fl state workers storming gov office #1HA #wheresswift

All us workers at the State House have fuckin had it. We're understaffed and Swift don't care. Twenty of us hammered on his door today demanding an answer before the cops turned up and threw us out. He said 1HA would bring in money and we'd get more employees to handle all these applications. It's been over a year and it ain't happened. Hell, he cut our budget again. Our manager's pissed and we are too. Where's that money? Where's it going? That fucker needs to give us more people or resign if he ain't up to the job.

American Criminology Society, March 2025: Evidence of bias found in administration of Florida's One Homicide Act

Last year, Florida passed a controversial law allowing each citizen one permissible homicide in their lifetime with no legal consequences. A comprehensive review of the One Homicide Act conducted by a team of criminologists, sociologists, and FBI agents, coordinated by the University of Florida's Department of Sociology, revealed surprising results.

The study surveyed all of the Intent to Murder applications filed in the space of one year, starting shortly after the law was passed.

The total amounted to over one hundred thousand, approximately thirty-nine percent of the state's population.

The vast majority of Intent to Murder applications, eighty-two percent, were filed by men. Of those, more than half applied to murder women. Ex-partners were the most common targets, followed by employers. Thirty percent of the applications to murder ex-spouses were denied due to "overly personal motives." All but five percent of the applications to murder female employers were approved.

The sociologist who organized the study says this points to a clear flaw in the One Homicide Act. "Our criminal justice system already favors the wealthy. The Florida law exacerbates this imbalance by allowing the privileged to further assert their dominance over the marginalized. Women only filed fourteen percent of applications, and over half got rejected. The applications of people of color are disproportionately rejected forty-one percent of the time, as opposed to twenty-two percent of white citizens' applications."

A criminologist who collaborated on the study raised similar concerns. "Background checks are either not conducted or are inconsistent. We selected a sample of two hundred approved applications submitted by men to murder ex-spouses. Of those applicants, more than half had prior arrests for domestic violence against their intended victims. This information is readily available through a basic criminal background check."

The authors of the study claimed they tried to schedule a meeting with Governor Mark Swift and state police chief Bernard Wayne to discuss the results. The governor did not respond, and Chief Wayne sent a form email saying the meeting was "unnecessary."

The study is available for free on the University website. The authors will also provide free copies upon request.

Facebook, Juan Rivera, March 9, 2025; with Darren Cohen

RECOMMENDATIONS NEEDED

So guys, I need a lawyer. Or my neighbor Darren does. A few days ago I got a target notice in the mail. It said Darren wanted to kill me. I was surprised because we've always had a good relationship. Not super tight but we always stop and talk when we run into each other. So I talked to him. I wanted to know what I did to upset him. He swore he never applied to kill me and I believed him. We both went to City Hall and he demanded to see the application. It was in his name so they had to show it to him. And it turns out that as the target I was allowed to see it too. Darren showed them his license and the ID on the application had a totally different picture. It was a dude I used to work with, Victor Preston. We talked to a manager and they said Victor had applied to kill me before. He said I got him fired. He got fired because he was harassing female customers. One woman got a restraining order against him. I just told the boss what he was doing. He applied to kill me before with his real name but it got rejected because he has two priors for assault. Doesn't surprise me, that dude is crazy.

So anyway, Darren's pressing charges against Victor for identity theft. And maybe suing the city for pushing the application through. If anybody knows a good lawyer in the Miami area, let me know. I used to support 1HA, now I'm not so sure.

Pro tip: if you're named as a target, go to City Hall and ask to see the application. If you ask, they have to show it to you. I don't think a lot of people know that. I didn't until yesterday.

Arizona Daily, March 27, 2025: Tucson man sues after IJA application rejection; legal experts warn of surge in civil suits in "murder law" states

Mitchell Barnes, a 48-year-old resident of Tucson, sued the city and the state of Arizona for rejecting his Individual Justice Act (IJA) application. The reviewer, junior director of the Department of IJA Enforcement, wrote in an email that she rejected the application because of "disturbing racist language. He wanted to kill a black man who happened to move into his neighborhood. He didn't provide any evidence of harassment or disturbances. He just said the intended target would 'bring trouble.' It was not, in my opinion, in keeping with the intent of IJA."

The Tucson city manager, who reviewed the application after Barnes' suit was filed, did not respond to requests for an interview. However, according to an anonymous source at City Hall, the city manager has expressed sympathy with Barnes and is pushing the city to settle.

Tom Newburg, a professor at the University of Arizona School of Law, says this suit is part of a larger trend. "The civil courts in Florida have been glutted with suits since the passing of the One Homicide Act. I predict the same thing will happen in Arizona."

"Arizona hasn't had time to set any precedent, and the language in their law is even vaguer and more open to loopholes than Florida's," said Margaret Nelson, a civil litigation attorney practicing in Tucson. "The state has already had two suits from people who said their IJA applications shouldn't have been denied. They were dismissed, but the procedures still slow down the courts. My office gets multiple calls about suits related to the Individual Justice Act every day. Some don't have merit but several do. In the name of 'freedom' and bending to the extreme libertarian faction of the population, Arizona is making a mockery of the rule of law."

Retired Pima County judge Pablo Hernandez expressed similar concerns. "My former colleagues have told me that their civil litigation dockets have almost doubled since IJA passed. I've never seen such a large increase in such a short period of time. At the very least, the law needs to be amended to tighten these loopholes." Hernandez and over fifty current and former Arizona judges signed a letter to Governor Max McCarthy asking for a review of the Individual Justice Act. A statement was released on Governor McCarthy's official X (formerly Twitter) page: "While I have sympathy for the judges' position, I believe that the Individual Justice Act is in no need of revision at this time. Any attempt at thwarting any infinite number of scenarios will only lead to more red tape, which IJA was designed to decrease."

Miami Tribune, April 3, 2025: Charges of One Homicide Act exploitation against Waterson dismissed

A Miami-Dade County judge dismissed the charges against Palmetto Construction Group CEO Harry Waterson, accused of exploiting the One Homicide Act for personal gain. Judge Garrett Bolling said in his ruling that the claim that Waterson paid employees to carry out murders on his behalf "cannot be proven." The employees who committed the murders will not be charged, since they were found to have acted lawfully under the One Homicide Act. However, their requests to have their legal homicides reinstated will not be granted. The employees, Judge Bolling said, "cannot prove they did not file the applications of their own free will. Therefore, these count as their one legal homicide."

The Florida ACLU attorneys for Waterson's employees said in an interview that they plan to appeal the ruling. "There's more evidence out there, something that can prove Waterson's ruthless exploitation of his employees. We will continue to fight to get them the justice they deserve and to get Waterson the prison cell he deserves."

Palm Beach Post, April 10, 2025: "Proxy defense" of 1HA target heads to circuit court

Elena Rubenstein received a victim notification that she had been targeted by Terrence Gambon, the former gardener of her and her husband, Noah Rubenstein. Rubenstein, who is a paraplegic and uses a wheelchair, told her husband and he took measures to protect her. He installed security cameras around their home and hired a driver to accompany Elena when she left their home.

Gambon's attorney argues that since Elena, the named victim, didn't defend against the attack, his client has not voided his right to attempt to kill her again. The Rubensteins' attorney argues that, since Elena's physical condition prohibited her from defending herself, her husband had the right to act on her behalf, thereby voiding any future murder attempt by Gambon.

Redacted, A Progressive Hacker Collective, Official Website, April 30, 2025: 1HA Experiment Results

Over the last two months, Redacted has been running an experiment on the One Homicide Act application process in Florida, after reading reports about biases in the system. Dedicated as we are to exposing cultural biases and injustices, we decided to put the theory to the test.

We reached out to members and followers in Florida and asked them to submit Intent to Murder applications. Several of these applications included blatant violations of the stated rules. One posed as a father applying to kill his daughter, giving the reason as

"She wouldn't cancel her trip to Europe to come to our anniversary dinner. And she broke up with a perfectly nice man who she coulda settled down with. She constantly finds ways to disappoint us." The written rules of 1HA clearly state that parents cannot apply to kill their children. Yet despite this, and the petty reason, the application was approved. The original applications and the corresponding approval or rejection letters, along with the complete text of the One Homicide Act, are linked below.

We had six men and four women fill out Intent to Murder applications. We know, not a comprehensive sample, but it was an exercise to test the findings of another study (linked below) that had a bigger sample and came to the same conclusion.

Three of the four women were rejected. It should be noted that the one woman's application that was approved was applying to kill a female victim, a woman she claimed had spread damaging rumors about her. Of the three women who were rejected, one applied to kill an abusive boyfriend, another a boss who sexually harassed her and fired her when she rejected his advances, and the last a male neighbor who drove into her house while drunk, causing thousands of dollars' worth of damage that he refused to pay. A male applicant who cited an almost identical motive to the last one was approved.

Even though "excessively personal motives" are officially forbidden by the rules, a male applicant who applied to kill a woman who wouldn't go on a second date with him was approved. He cited "severe emotional trauma and theft of money, cause I paid for dinner" as the motive.

It should also be noted that the one male applicant who was rejected gave his profession as a legal assistant at the Florida Minority Legal Defense Fund. He applied to kill a lawyer who had defended an off-duty cop charged with shooting a black man on his lawn. This is a real story BTW. It's linked below. We just changed the names of the people involved.

Something else worth noting: Every target name on the applications in our experiment was fake. And several were still approved. So there is obviously a serious flaw in even the most basic fact checking in the review process.

After receiving their approval notification, each applicant sent an official notice rescinding their application (which is allowed under the law), explaining the experiment. None of them received any kind of response from any Florida state official.

We are in the process of organizing a similar experiment in Arizona and are still seeking volunteers. Click here for more info.

TikTok, @jose_torres_azlatinx, May 15, 2025: #IJA Update

Hey everybody, bad news. My IJA application got rejected.

Recap in case you missed it: I applied to kill Miguel Ramirez, one of the assholes at my school who's been beating up my brother Hector and making his life hell. The school hasn't done a damn thing to help him. Miguel's parents make excuses for him. If they had done their jobs I wouldn't have to do this. But they didn't, so I had to step in. But the dickheads at Mesa City Hall rejected my application. They said I "couldn't prove any bodily harm." My mother and I called, and after being on hold for almost thirty minutes, the bitch on the other end said that I had to prove that Miguel was hurting me. So I guess I can only kill somebody if they're hurting me. That's bullshit.

If you hurt my brother, you hurt me. I hate watching Hector suffer like this. He can't wait three years to take care of it himself. He might not live that long. If you saw what that bastard has done to him, you'd know I'm serious. Miguel Ramirez is a bully and a psycho and the world is better off without him. My mom is trying to find a lawyer to see if we can appeal. I'll have updates as they come.

David Hume Official Site, May 21, 2025: Response to Pro-Choice America

Representatives of Pro-Choice America contacted me to voice their concerns about the effect of the One Homicide Act on women's reproductive rights. Thank you for bringing this to my attention. I have fought for Florida women's right to choose during my time in office, often in the face of virulent opposition, and will continue to do so. I am currently reviewing possible remedies to 1HA to address this issue while preserving the integrity of the law.

Facebook, Ellen Wasserbach, June 1, 2025

I got an IJA target notice in my email today. Not gonna lie, I'm fucking scared.

Thank you to everybody who stood by me, for all the recommendations for self-defense training and security measures. If I survive until next year, I'm buying you all a drink.

If I die, know that I love you. To honor my memory, do everything you can to get rid of this cruel law. If I survive, that's exactly what I'm gonna do. Nobody else should have to feel what I'm feeling now.

Florida Socialist Collective, Official Website, June 17, 2025: 1HA Another Capitalist Boot on the Neck of the People

When I first read about the One Homicide Act, I actually thought it could be a good thing. We could take out the rich bastards with the same impunity from the totalitarian police state they've always enjoyed. If each of us revolutionaries killed just one of those assholes we could topple the entrenched system and finally make real change. But, spoiler alert, the overfed robber barons are beating the system like they always do. They can't ask for help from their old buddies the police but they can throw their money at security systems and bodyguards. Because if they stop an attack they aren't held accountable. I mean they never are but it's literally written into the law. I think you can try again before the year is up but once that time is up you can't apply to kill them again. One more way American "justice" favors the rich. Hume says it's equal but that's bullshit. Nothing is truly equal under capitalism.

My application to kill the bastard developer who tore down my apartment building, one of the few affordable places left in Orlando, got approved. I said he forced me out of my home and took away my livelihood. Which is true. Gentrification and late-stage capitalism are doing that to millions across the country.

I staked out the dude's mansion on the edge of town, far away from the common people he screws over. It's a fucking fortress. I watch his security, take notes, plan my attack. When I was ready I got past the censors around the gate and was on my way to the garage. I knew he was heading out that night, probably to some fundraiser with his rich bastard friends. I get to the garage and run into a brick wall of a security guard. He drops me with one punch. I don't remember much after that but I woke up in an ambulance. Surprised they didn't just leave me in the street.

The point is, if those bastards came after us we couldn't afford anything like that to protect ourselves. They can kill us far more easily than we can kill them. It was all supposed to be equal but of course it isn't. It's another rigged system in favor of the rich.

I'm not saying we should stop trying. One of these bastards has to let their guard down eventually. Then we'll be there. If just one falls they'll know they haven't defeated us. That we can and will fight back.

Tallahassee Observer, June 20, 2025: Target notification provision of One Homicide Act upheld at State House

The state legislature held an emergency vote yesterday on a provision in the One Homicide Act that informs prospective victims, or targets, named in murder applications. The provision, rushed through committee after news of a group of high school students were charged with sending falsified target notices, remained in place after a 62-38 vote. State representative Dana Holbrook said in support of the provision, "The One Homicide Act requires transparency to function properly. Victims have a right to know when they're being targeted."

The vote was called by Senator Jerome Rhodes. In support, Rhodes cited stories of ten separate incidents of notified targets murdering their killers. "Not one of them was in immediate danger. They set out to murder these people, and will face no legal consequences. Some of the methods they used were horrific."

Jose Morena, a Miami-area public defender, countered, "I believe we can extend the definition of self-defense to someone who has been named as a target for murder. Even if they are not being physically harmed at that moment, they know they will be at some point. They are preventing harm to themselves. That is the essence of self-defense."

Laura Young, spokesperson for Stop the Cycle, an anti-1HA advocacy group, cited the controversy as an example of why the law should be repealed. "It has not decreased crime. If anything, it's lead to more murders, all committed without consequence.

The easiest way to resolve this issue is to simply do away with the law."

Governor Mark Swift and State Senator David Hume did not respond to requests for comment.

Criminal Justice Journal, July 2025: Domestic violence incidents rise in Florida in the wake of the One Homicide Act

Six months after touting a report that the One Homicide Act has led to lower crime, including a decrease in domestic violence, a study of Florida police records from four major cities (Miami, Orlando, Jacksonville, and Tampa) show a rise in reports of domestic violence. Jacksonville saw a twenty-two percent rise in reports, Miami seventeen percent, Orlando thirteen percent, and Tampa eleven percent.

A review of Intent to Murder applications reveals that thirty-four percent of the victims filing the reports had also filed applications to kill their abusers. Half of these applications were rejected citing "excessively personal motives." Of the applications that were accepted, almost half resulted in failed attempts with the intended victims defending themselves, which, according to the provisions of the law, meant that the applicants could not apply to kill the intended victims again.

One police report states that the aggressor was so enraged by his wife's attempt to kill him that he locked her in the garage overnight. She reported the incident the next day after breaking free.

Arizona Daily, August 2, 2025: Former state employee alleges fraud in IJA enforcement

Lucia Carreras, a former employee at Tempe City Hall, alleges that there has been significant fraud in the Individual Justice Act, a law passed last year that allows each Arizona resident to commit one officially sanctioned homicide without legal consequences. The allegations were listed in an affidavit for her wrongful termination suit against the city of Tempe.

Carreras says she was fired last month for approving an application for a woman who named her ex-husband as a target. "It followed all the rules, I could verify the identities of both the applicant and the target, so I approved it. Then it turned out the ex-husband was a friend of a state senator, so my boss said it had to be rejected. That was exactly what he said. There was no room for interpretation. He said, 'Senator Bryson wants this application denied.' I refused, and four days later I got fired. They said it was because of budget cuts, but I know that's not true. My friend who still works there says they're interviewing for my replacement. There are no budget cuts."

A spokesperson for Tempe City Hall dismissed Carreras' allegations, saying, "Ms. Carreras was the lowest performing employee in her group in a time of budget cuts. As a disgruntled former employee, she should not be taken seriously." A review of the Tempe city budget reveals an increase in funds to hire new employees, specifically citing an increased work load due to the Individual Justice Act.

The Governor's office did not respond to requests for comment.

FeminismNews.org, August 16, 2025: Pro-Choice America suit against Florida shot down by state Supreme Court

Earlier this year, the Florida chapter of Pro-Choice America filed a lawsuit against the state of Florida, citing the number of abortion doctors being murdered under the One Homicide Act, as well as women who were murdered by partners and family members after having abortions. They claimed the murders violated the provisions of the law, stating that excessively personal motives were prohibited. "What's more excessively personal than interfering with a woman's bodily autonomy?"

The State Supreme Court dismissed the suit. "Physicians are not public figures. While the issue of abortion is a highly politicized one and stirs deep emotions in both supporters and opponents, after a review of the applications and the murders, it is my opinion that the killings did not violate the law."

State Senator David Hume, architect of the One Homicide Act, did not respond to requests for comments.

You Tube Vlogger Retribution89, August 31, 2025: "1HA Kill of the Week"

Our Kill of the Week comes to us from Howie Young out of Gainesville. Dude got disrespected by some cuck at a bar at Florida U. Howie was just tryin to enlighten him and the dude shoved him aside, got him kicked out of the bar. Anyways he gets to cuck's dorm and blasts him at the door. Got a video of him hittin the pavement. You can hear his skull crack. Awesome. Pussy boy really does have shit for brains now. Howie's gonna get a prize. Get in your best kills for a chance to be on the show. Don't forget to like and subscribe.

Reality Check: An Alternative Journalism Source, September 8, 2025: Are state economies really thriving under murder laws?

Florida's claims of a spike in tourism following the passage of the One Homicide Act needs a reality check. While it is true that tourism has increased, they left out a key detail. Longtime residents are leaving the state in droves. According to state tax records, Florida's population has dropped by almost five thousand since the beginning of 2024, when the One Homicide Act went into effect. And it isn't just that more people are getting murdered. Ever since the Murder Law passed, at least four thousand residents have moved out of Florida. Many of them moved just over the state line to Georgia. So yes, more people are coming to Florida. But they're not staying.

The same thing happened in Arizona. After passing the Individual Justice Act last year, approximately fifteen hundred Arizona residents relocated to New Mexico or California based on postal records.

Even the murder tourists touted by supporters aren't exactly coming out of admiration. We've curated a file of over one hundred social media posts from visitors to Florida and Arizona (link here), and they are far from complimentary. One California resident visiting Arizona wrote on Bluesky: "I had to go to Phoenix for work and the whole place is giving serious Mad Max with #IJA. I was just walking along, heard a gunshot and this guy fell down dead across the street. Everybody just kept walking. I'd be low-key scared all the time if I lived here."

With murder laws in the pipeline in other states like Alabama and Nevada, the novelty for murder tourism will wear off. The current murder law states won't even have tourism money to make up for the lost tax revenue of the thousands of residents leaving.

Reddit, r/Arizona, September 12, 2025: "The people working on IJA applications need to get their shit together"

My IJA application got rejected because they said I already used my murder. I definitely didn't. Someone in Mesa with the same name used hers, and whoever reviewed my application thought it was me. Seriously, they didn't run the Social Security number? I've been trying to get it straightened out but nobody at City Hall picks up the phone. I was on hold for over an hour yesterday. Same thing with the IJA help line at the State House. Hey, if I can't use my murder, I'll ultimately be okay with it. The asshole deserves it, but it's not like I have to kill him. But how many other applicants got rejected, or people getting approved who shouldn't, because the Arizona govt can't get its shit together? Has anybody been able to get through to them? Please, I need all the help I can get.

Florida Supreme Court Docket, September 30, 2025: Decision in Rubenstein v. Florida

"The plaintiff was well within his rights to defend his wife. Mrs. Rubenstein, the plaintiff's wife, due to circumstances beyond her control, was unable to properly defend herself. Mrs. Rubenstein is in a wheelchair and therefore was unable to run for help or find another method to fight off her attacker, who was advancing on her with a knife when her husband, the plaintiff, intervened. The plaintiff stated that he did not mean to kill the attacker, Mr. Gambon. Medical evidence confirms this fact. Mr. Gambon, according to testimony from the medical examiner, was cut by his own knife in the struggle, slicing his carotid artery. Emergency personnel arrived too late to save him. We conclude that the plaintiff was well within his rights to take action against Mr. Gambon under the laws of the state of Florida to defend his wife from harm. As such, the plaintiff, Noah Rubenstein, still has the right to redeem his lawful murder under the One Homicide Act in the future, as does Elena Rubenstein."

National Gun Rights Alliance, October 4, 2025: Discounts for Murder Law states

NGRA supports murder laws. We spent funds and time supporting the One Homicide Act in Florida, and the Individual Justice Act in Arizona. These laws, like the Second Amendment, give the masses the power to fight back against tyranny.

Gun sales are up in murder law states. Membership in NGRA is up among residents in those states. The more armed citizens, the more we send a message to the oppressive government that we will fight back against them.

Click here for a list of gun retailers in Florida, Arizona and New Hampshire offering discounts for Murderers and Targets. Show your notices and get up to 30 percent off guns and ammo. Protect yourselves and your rights.

Austin Sun, October 12, 2025: Volunteer Executioner Act goes to General Assembly

The controversial Volunteer Executioner Act, introduced by State Assembly Member Aaron Gilmore, will begin debates today in the Assembly chamber. The law, endorsed by Governor Ted Newman and supported by seventy-one percent of polled citizens, would allow state residents to carry out the executions of Death Row inmates on a volunteer basis.

The local chapter of the ACLU condemned the measure. "This will continue the glorification of the barbaric practice of capital punishment," a spokesperson said.

Gilmore's office responded to the criticism in an email to this reporter. "Capital punishment is a crucial part of the criminal justice system. The Volunteer Execution Act will involve the people in this vital process."

The law is seen as Newman's promised revamping of the controversial "murder laws" recently passed in Florida and Arizona. Gilmore's office said, "The biggest problem with those laws is that they target innocent victims. Our Volunteer Execution program will fix that, and close the numerous loopholes that created so many problems in those states. It will also save taxpayers millions of dollars a year. The current execution system requires a team of multiple people to carry out one death sentence."

The Volunteer Execution Act will appear on the ballot in a special election next month, where it is expected to pass.

Reddit, r/AZ IJA: Buy my murder

If you've already used your murder or you don't live in Arizona and want to kill someone who lives here you can have my murder. Officially murders aren't transferrable. But there are ways around that. They never actually check if the person who submitted the application is the one doing the killing. How could they? The applicant just loses their murder.

I have no intention of using my murder. Don't need it, don't want it. For 500 dollars minimum or best offer, tell me who you want killed and why and I'll apply to kill them. Pay me upon approval of the application. Then you can kill them and I'll fill out the completion paperwork online. DM me for details.

Florida Bar Association, Official Website, October 23, 2025: Editorial: The One Homicide Act Needs to Be Repealed

Case after case has exposed glaring and dangerous loopholes in the law, with little to nothing being done to close them. If anything, the few actions taken increase the risk to the population and the potential for exploitation. The state of Florida, and other areas of the country, see decreasing crime statistics on a piece of paper without considering the human cost of "law and order." This attitude has created a dangerous atmosphere for large segments of the population, and the One Homicide Act is perpetuating it. The Florida Bar Association calls on Governor Mark Swift and the state legislature, as well as the voters of Florida, to repeal this inhumane and poorly executed measure.

Orlando Sun, October 26, 2025: Hume proposes One Homicide Act amendments

State Senator David Hume, in response to overwhelming public pressure to change the One Homicide Act, introduced amendments to the controversial law in committee today. The new language would include mandatory psychological screening for applicants, as well as thorough background checks of applicants and victims. Hume's new provisions state that the victim had to have caused harm to person or property, or made the murderer feel unsafe in any way. "It came to my attention that applications were being approved for men to murder women who simply ignored them in a bar one night," Hume says. "That is not acceptable."

In addition, Hume will reintroduce a previously proposed amendment protecting abortion providers. "After careful examination, I believe it falls under the 'excessively personal' motive."

Governor Mark Swift's office has not given any indication on whether the governor will sign the bill. Swift's office previously spoke against psychological screening of applicants, calling it "unrealistic." Swift, who has supported increasingly restrictive anti-abortion measures, has already said he will veto any form of the bill with protection for abortion doctors. Hume, however, believes he can "get the votes" to override a veto.

Governor Swift's office did not respond to requests for comment.

San Antonio Chronicle, November 3, 2025: Volunteer Executioner Act opponent attacked in parking lot

Walt Lehman, president of the Texas Chapter of Citizens for Criminal Justice Reform (CCJR) appeared on San Antonio's Channel 6 News Tuesday evening, encouraging Texans to vote against the popular yet controversial Volunteer Executioner Act. The following day, he was attacked in a parking lot by a masked assailant.

Lehman is expected to make a full recovery. He gave an interview to this publication from his hospital room, where he continued to speak out against the Volunteer Execution Act. "The attack on me is just another symptom of this state's, this country's disease. We worship violence. We believe that without violence, there is no justice. But that's wrong. We're the only first world country that still practices the death penalty and we're mocked and shamed around the world for it. Having citizens act as executioners will only exacerbate the issue."

San Antonio police say they are currently seeking Lehman's attacker, but would not provide further details.

TheWatcher.net, A Guerilla News Network, November 6, 2025: Confessions of a Murder Photographer

I live in Arizona, and I posted pictures of an IJA murder I happened to catch on Reddit. Then a guy in Florida who was doing the same thing showed me how to set up a subscription site and make some money. I was making jack shit as a wedding and event photographer so I did it. But now I'm done. I just can't do it anymore.

The first one was in Scottsdale. I was in the right place at the right time. Some dude was in my neighborhood. He looked kind of shady, so I took out my camera and got some footage in case he did something shady. He walked up to a nearby house, knocked on the door, and then just stabbed the person who answered the door. And then he just walked away and took out his phone, talking on it while standing in front of the house watching this woman bleed to death. Then I realized it was an IJA murder.

While he waited for the police to get him, I managed to get a couple shots of the body. I posted it on Reddit and it went viral. It felt good. I wanted more.

The photographer in Florida, don't ask me his name, I only know his online handle, told me how to get more business. I contacted people on the IJA forum on Reddit who got approved for murders and offered my services. They told me where the murder was gonna go down, I went, took video, and emailed it to them. They didn't see me or know my real name. Made good money.

But after a while it got depressing, and scary. I looked up the law and there is no restriction on how you're allowed to kill. You can use hardcore torture, whatever. And some people really take advantage of it. But I kept doing it cause it was such good money. And because I thought that if these people were getting killed they must have done something bad. After all the applications got approved so they had to have a good reason to kill. But then I videoed one murder that fucking broke me. Don't ask what happened. Just don't. I deleted the footage and refunded the guy's money. I did not want to be tied to him in any way. I wish I could delete it from my memory.

I wrote a letter to my state senator saying IJA needs to be repealed. It's seriously bringing out the worst in people. Including me.

Houston Sun, November 7, 2025: Volunteer Executioner Act approved in landslide vote

Texas voters approved the controversial Volunteer Executioner Act by a margin of eighty-two percent. Introduced by Governor Newman and drafted by State Delegate Gilmore, the measure would allow state residents to carry out death sentences on prisoners awaiting execution. Gilmore says the inspiration came from Florida's One Homicide Act, but "using it in a more lawful way."

Rosa Otero, president of Restoring Justice, an Austin-based legal advocacy group, gave an interview on Austin This Morning expressing her disagreement with the new law. "We already know the current system for capital punishment has multiple flaws. Allowing citizens with no knowledge of the legal process to murder their fellow citizens is barbaric. This will not deter crime. It will only further glorify violence in our society."

The state police union has voiced support for the Volunteer Execution Act, calling it a "relief on the tax burden of carrying out vital death sentences that provide closure to victims and ensure compliance with the law." The same union official, however, is opposed to Florida's One Homicide Act, which Gilmore cited as his inspiration. "The people simply can't be trusted to take the law into their own hands on that level. Especially with so little oversight. Texas' law will have stricter provisions and we know those getting killed absolutely deserve it."

Gilmore, after the deciding vote, said, "This is a great day for Texas. The new law will lower taxes and give our residents a first-hand look at justice being served."

Concord Times, November 8, 2025: New Hampshire passes Correction Act

In yesterday's special election, the Correction Act passed sixty-three to thirty-seven. The hotly contested law allows residents to kill one person with no legal consequences, provided their applications are approved by a specially selected committee of legal professionals. The Correction Act was inspired by the One Homicide Act in Florida and the Individual Justice Act in Arizona, collectively referred to as "murder laws."

State Senator Thomas Loeb introduced the Correction Act on the legislature floor earlier this year, where he claimed that he had "carefully considered all the issues in Florida and Arizona," and pledges to have a proposal "as free of loopholes as possible."

In a statement after the law's passing, Loeb promised to pay particular attention to the reported gender biases in Florida's enactment of the law. "Domestic violence and assault victims need the Correction Act more than anyone. This law implements a rigorous screening procedure to give priority to victims of bureaucratic oversight in the legal system, victims of criminals who got off on technicalities. Extra priority will be given to victims of domestic and sexual crimes who were denied justice."

Loeb says the governing statutes for the Correction Act will be drafted this week.

Florida Democratic Party, Official Website, November 11, 2025: Why we will fight the Senate Republicans' new 1HA proposal

State Senator Phyllis Taylor announced today that she would be introducing a new amendment to the One Homicide Act on the floor tomorrow. Her proposal would make the already abhorrent 1HA even more dangerous. Taylor, a crony of Governor Swift (her husband used to work with him), wants to include a protection of so-called "high-value residents" against being killed under the law. Swift, naturally, has expressed his support.

How is "high value" defined by Taylor? Annual income. Any resident with more than $500,000 in annual income will be automatically exempt from being killed under the law. As is the GOP standard, the rich are worth more than everybody else.

Tampa Bay Post, November 22, 2025: Senate enacts target notice amendment, rejects other proposed 1HA amendments

Under a new amendment to the controversial One Homicide Act, a target notified under the One Homicide Act cannot seek out their prospective murderer. They can only kill the murderer if they are being attacked or about to be attacked. The new provision is in response to both the debate around the Proxy Defense and reports of a target who murdered his future killer being denied his own murder. "A target cannot take extra measures like this in defense. They have to be in immediate danger for self-defense to apply," Senator Paul Randolph said in the hearing.

An amendment proposed to restrict murder methods, supported by 1HA architect David Hume, did not pass committee. "The law is about freedom. Methodology is arbitrary and shouldn't be restricted based on whether one person might find it immoral or excessive. These things are in the eyes of the beholder," Senator Randolph wrote on X (formerly Twitter). "It's sad to see Senator Hume abandon his principles to buckle to the hurt feelings of a minority."

Hume responded in a statement on his website: "Freedom is everybody having the right to defend themselves and be equal under the law. It does not apply to the vicious murder methods that some Florida residents have come up with. State records show that some 1HA targets have been tortured for days before being killed. I've learned in the last two years that there should be some restrictions on personal freedom. The good among us need to be protected from the bad."

Governor Mark Swift's office said in an official statement: "The arbitrary and frankly unenforceable restriction on murder methods is not in keeping with the spirit of the One Homicide Act, and I was happy to see the Senate reject it."

However, in a blow to the Florida GOP, Sen. Phyllis Taylor's amendment to ban killing of "high value" residents was rejected, despite support from Gov. Swift. Hume was among the opponents, releasing a statement on X before the vote: "1HA is supposed to be accessible to all Floridians. The wealthy so-called 'high-value' residents have more than enough resources to defend themselves. They do not need additional protection from the government." Gov. Swift and Sen. Taylor have not commented on the amendment's failure.

GoFundMe, November 29, 2025: Help me open my murder park

Hey guys, I have a great plan for Arizona. A murder park. A lot of places have banned IJA murders, and we need a place to exercise our rights. Buy a piece of land, keep the location private and only available via invitation so targets won't know what's happening. Have some other stuff there to throw off the scent. Charge admission for people to watch and take pictures.

I need some startup money for the plans. Donate what you can and you'll get free admission.

Psychology Today, December 6, 2025: Mental health professionals continue to question ethics of "murder laws"

In an editorial in the most recent edition of *Journal of Clinical Psychology*, Miami-area psychologist Brenda Blake criticized Florida's controversial One Homicide Act. Dr. Blake argues that the law's provision that the victim be notified of being named as a target in an Intent to Murder application is causing prospective victims, or "targets", "life-crippling stress."

"We now have thousands of people constantly on edge because they're worried they will be attacked at any moment" and says she and other area therapists have seen a spike in new patients as a result. "This law has created a mental health crisis in the state."

Dr. Blake's comments join a growing movement among mental health professionals raising ethical questions about the so-called "murder laws" currently in effect in Florida, Arizona, and New Hampshire.

"I fear this law will give some troubled people an easy out. If they are allowed to murder someone who they feel is creating their problems, it prevents them from confronting their issues and truly healing," Dr. Amir Nasam, a psychiatry professor at the University of Arizona, said in an interview with this writer.

A therapist in Orlando, speaking anonymously, agreed. "Revenge is outward facing. True healing requires looking inward. This law is giving people an excuse to not look at themselves but instead turn their focus to others who may not deserve it." He says he had a patient who committed suicide shortly after being notified as a victim. "I think the stress was just too much for her."

The American Psychological Association, who published an editorial in their newsletter one month after the passing of the One Homicide Act in January 2024, has sent formal letters to the governors of Florida, Arizona, and New Hampshire, as well as other states considering "murder laws", urging reconsideration and repeal.

A statement published in the APA Journal summarized the concerns of mental health professionals: "The current screening process is not enough. No psychological tests are conducted to ensure that the applicants are of sound mind. And, as several studies and testimony reveal, even the most basic background checks are not always properly conducted. At the very least, the current system needs to be revised. We want the law repealed, but if you refuse to do that, at least institute thorough psychological screenings of applicants."

A spokesperson for Florida Governor Mark Swift wrote in an email to this reporter: "We understand the concerns surrounding this law. But what the APA is asking is unrealistic. We simply don't have the time or resources to conduct evaluations on the hundreds of homicide applicants. At some point, we have to trust the citizens to regulate themselves. The crime statistics speak for themselves. This measure is working, and the state sees no reason to change it at this time."

The offices of the governors of Arizona and New Hampshire did not respond to requests for comment.

Variety, January 19, 2026: Filmmakers and studios may stop filming in Florida and other "murder law" states

In 2023, Florida passed the "One Homicide Act." It allows each state resident to murder one person in their lifetime without facing criminal charges. It has been highly controversial, yet sixty-two percent of Florida residents support it according to a recent poll.

Arizona and New Hampshire passed similar "murder laws," and other states are reportedly considering similar legislation.

The law has generated a lot of press. Here in Hollywood, it's given several filmmakers pause about filming in the Sunshine State.

Florida is an attractive filming location for many reasons; tax incentives on top of already low tax rates, warm weather year-round, attractive scenery, and plenty of natural light. But the so-called "murder law" has studios weighing insurance risks, and filmmakers fearful for their lives. While the law states that victims as well as murderers must be Florida residents, recent reports indicate lax enforcement of the rules.

Even if the stars and director aren't at risk, many filmmakers and studios are wondering if the possibility of a legal murder taking place on or near the set could pose a liability issue.

"I've filmed in Florida, and always hire local crew. What if one of them gets killed on set? We have security but what if somebody gets through? And what about when they go home?" one TV director said. "One thing's for sure, I am not filming in Florida while the murder law is in effect."

Several filmmakers and actors echoed these concerns. An independent film director who was planning to shoot his current project in Florida says he's decided to move production to Georgia. Agents report that many of their clients have added clauses to their contracts saying they will not film in states with "murder laws."

Variety reached out to government officials in Florida for comment, but did not receive responses.

TikTok, @onwednesdayswesmashthepatriarchy, February 17, 2026: Fuck #1HA and its ableist bullshit

Hey y'all, ya girl in Tampa here fighting the good fight in this blood red state. Literally. Florida has fully entered its supervillain era. Seriously, y'all won't believe this latest dose of bullshit courtesy of 1HA.

The facts of this story would be fuckin wild if they weren't also so fuckin sad. This bitch, right here in Tampa, naming and shaming, sorry not sorry, Roberta Rogan, got the green light to kill her disabled stepson. She got around the "can't kill your kids" rule because she wasn't his biological mother. Her reason? He was a financial burden. Not his fault. Her husband, Greg Rogan, is a fucking millionaire. I know them. See them around all the fuckin time. And he's a big Republican donor. Roberta's Instagram is full of all the new designer clothes she just bought. It's all right here in the link. Check out my profile for the full link list. Maybe use a fraction of the money you spent buying politicians and overpriced sweatshop produced clothes to take care of your fucking child. Y'all just didn't wanna take care of him. Didn't want the shame of having a disabled child. Roberta posts her mini-me daughter all the time, but never a fucking word about her stepson.

Maybe if Fuhrer Swift hadn't cut the budget for disability services, look it up, link right here, he wouldn't'a been a financial burden.

And her husband, the kid's biological father, just looked the other way. Did nothing to protect his son from his literal wicked stepmother. Who else thinks he was the real brains behind this plan? He couldn't do it because of the parents can't kill kids rule. He got a woman to do his dirty work like so many asshole men. It's right there in the name, smash the patriarchy. And repeal 1HA. Or at least use it to take out the sexists and capitalists destroying the world.

Criminal Justice Journal, February 22, 2026: The One Homicide Act and Overcrowding in Prisons: Abstract

Florida Governor Mark Swift claimed the One Homicide Act would alleviate overcrowding in prisons. Florida has the third highest per capita prison population in the country. Swift claimed that by allowing citizens to each kill one person in their lifetime, the prison population would go down. He cited "evolutionary psychologist" Benjamin Vandrake, whose degree came from an unaccredited online university, who claims that crime comes from "man's primitive urges left with no outlet in modern society." The One Homicide Act, Swift said, would give an outlet to that primitive urge, as well as "clean up the errors liberal judges and public defenders have wrought on our justice system."

Two years is too short a time for a complete analysis, but preliminary reports suggest that Governor Swift's predictions were incorrect. A review of new inmates sentenced to Florida prisons since the passing of the One Homicide Act shows no decrease. In fact, 2025 saw a slight increase from the year before of approximately 10,000 new inmates.

This study will look at the possible factors driving the increase in Florida's prison population, and whether it is related to the One Homicide Act.

Miami Underground, February 28, 2026: Editorial: Swift sheds last thread of respectability in latest press conference

Yesterday, the Florida legislature voted down a measure to have the sets of visiting filmmakers protected as "safe areas" from 1HA murders. Governor Mark Swift said in a press conference: "What makes the Hollywood elite think they deserve special treatment under our laws? If you want the privilege of filming in Florida, you respect our laws. You know movie studios are already coming here to be free from predatory California taxes. Look at the numbers. Our economy doesn't need you."

And with that statement, Swift has abandoned any pretense of being a respectable public figure. He has descended into the swamp of the worst of his constituents, crowing about "freedom" with no care for anyone their swinging limbs hit along the way. As long as that "freedom" only applies to white cis-gendered straight men like him. His record is anti-gay, anti-woman, anti-poor, anti-anybody not like him and his rich donors.

NPR.org, March 18, 2026: Florida governor under fire after online document leak

An anonymous source claiming to be a former member of Florida Governor Mark Swift's staff released damning documents on the social media website Reddit under the subreddit "Floridians Against 1HA." The source claims to have been in meetings with the governor where they discussed the state's controversial One Homicide Act. The law, which allows each Florida resident to murder one person without legal consequences, passed two years ago with 68 percent of the vote, and has been the subject of intense debates in Florida and around the country. Arizona and New Hampshire passed so-called "murder laws" in the 2024 elections, and Texas officials cited Florida's law as the inspiration for its Volunteer Executioner Act. However, Oregon defeated a proposed murder law in the recent midterm election, with polled voters calling it "scary."

The leaked documents show that the "experts" Swift met with were not law enforcement or scholars, but members of the Stirner Society, a self-described "total freedom advocacy group." 1HA architect David Hume, by his own admission, was once a member of the group, but distanced himself before beginning his political career. Governor Swift, while never an official member, is a close associate of the Florida chapter's president Gavin Dalton, a prominent real estate mogul who has contributed over one million dollars to Swift's campaign fund.

The source goes on to say that Swift had "personal reasons" for signing the law. According to the Redditor going by the screen name "cassandraoftheunderworld", "[Swift] killed someone right after the law passed."

After the leaked documents went public, another former staffer, posting under the screen name "kafkasnightmare," not only confirmed the allegations but added, "I filled out an Intent to Murder application for him. I didn't kill the guy but they needed a new person to do the application. He asked a lot of us to do that. Him or his chief of staff." When asked who "he" referred to, the anonymous source confirmed, "Swift. He's probably killed at least four by now. He used up his one murder, we all knew about it. He used it as an example in a staff meeting. And according to the law it has to be on public record. Though some people say he lied on his application. Then he called us all into his office and told us to do applications for people we'd never even heard of. Then I think he hired someone to kill them. Well that dude was dead and nobody was about to say Swift did it so the secret was safe."

Governor Swift's office did not respond to requests for comment.

Florida.gov, Office of the Governor, March 19, 2026: Governor responds to NPR article

In response to the baseless slander published by NPR this morning, I can assure the people of Florida that it is absolutely not true. We are disappointed that the once respected publication has lowered its journalistic standards. Their "source," Reddit.com, is a cesspool of amoral rabble rousers and unreliable hearsay. If necessary, I will take legal action against this disgusting libel.

Latin American League of Phoenix Official Website, April 2, 2026: Racial bias evident in IJA

Today we filed a lawsuit against the State of Arizona due to clear bias in the enforcement of the Individual Justice Act. Several citizens have contacted our office since IJA was passed, claiming their applications were rejected even though followed all the rules. Some said that almost identical applications were approved when the applicants were white. We obtained over three hundred applications through the Freedom of Information Act, and white people's applications were approved at a far higher rate than those of any minority groups, but particularly Latinx applicants. With this evidence in place, and the testimony of so far forty-two Latinx citizens, we are taking action against the state of Arizona and demanding justice under a law that denies it to us."

Miami Tribune, April 30, 2026: Amended One Homicide Act voted down in Assembly, critics cite "tax costs"

State Senator David Hume, architect of the One Homicide Act, introduced an amendment to his controversial law that would require a state-appointed psychologist to assess each applicant. "The application review process has become far too quick, and Governor Mark Swift is largely to blame for that. He's bowing to public pressure for fast results. I still believe in the One Homicide Act, but it needs to be applied carefully to be effective."

Opponents cited the tax costs for employing psychologists, which Hume refuted. "The State already has mental health professionals on staff. Hiring two or three more to assess 1HA applicants would be taken out of the state employee budget. It wouldn't raise taxes."

Hume's comments didn't stop the Republican majority Senate from naming cost as the primary reason for voting down the proposed amendment. One senator voiced another common concern: "The last thing we need is more red tape. The application process works as it is. Florida citizens deserve to take advantage of our newfound freedom without having to jump through bureaucratic hoops."

Hume's proposal to add abortion as a "political" motive was another "sticking point" in the amendment, according to a source in the State House. "They don't want to get on Swift's bad side. He has a lot of sway in the Florida Republican party. If they don't vote the way he want, they know they'll get primaried. And since Swift is very much allied with the pro-life lobby, Republicans don't want to be seen as soft on that issue."

A representative of Governor Swift wrote in an email: "The Governor supports the freedoms awarded to all citizens under the One Homicide Act and condemns the killing of unborn children. The Governor was happy with today's vote preserving the freedom of Floridians from invasive psychological tests and the right to protest the immoral practice of abortion."

Salt Lake Bugle, May 4, 2026: Sen. Jeffries to introduce "Atonement Act" in next session

Yesterday, State Representative Boyd Jeffries released a statement outlining the "Atonement Act." The law would allow each Utah resident to commit one homicide without legal consequences. While similar to other measures passed around the country, starting with Florida's One Homicide Act in 2023, Jeffries says his proposal is "not another murder law."

"Florid and Arizona's laws are anarchy," Jeffries said in his statement. "The state just takes the applicants' word for it that the reasons for killing are sound. We've all read the stories. Florida had a good idea but completely mismanaged it. There were no objective standards. And Arizona has almost no standards in enforcement at all. Under the Atonement Act, applicants have to prove themselves to be of sound mind and provide solid reasons for why they feel they need to commit this extreme act. A panel of experts will evaluate each applicant. I anticipate that only a fraction of applicants will be approved under the strict guidelines we will put in place."

Representative Jeffries' office did not respond to an email request for clarification on who will be included in the "panel of experts."

An insider at the State House told this reporter that the measure is likely to pass. "Almost all Republicans are in favor of it. One said it was a return to the pioneer days. A return to our heritage."

While similar laws in Florida, Arizona, and New Hampshire enjoyed initial popularity and resulted in declining crime rates, studies suggest that not only have they fallen out of favor with voters, but the touted results were at best short-lived. A study from a criminal justice journal found that domestic violence reports increased in Florida after the passage of the One Homicide Act. Arizona's Individual Justice Act has been the subject of numerous lawsuits alleging bias and corruption in its enforcement. In a post on X (formerly Twitter), Jeffries said, "I have carefully reviewed the results from FL, AZ, and NH. The Atonement Act will take all of those states' failings into account and try to correct them."

The Church State Separation Alliance (CSSA) has vowed to challenge the Atonement Act in court if it passes. A representative of the CSSA said in an interview with this reporter that Jeffries' statement makes "direct allusions" to Mormonism's "blood atonement," which the CSSA believes violates the separation clause. "This is blatantly unconstitutional," the representative said, "even in a borderline theocracy like Utah. Just because many of the citizens are the same religion does not give them the right to invoke religion in state law."

Jeffries did not respond to an email asking about the CSSA's charges of religious bias.

Facebook, Keisha Jones, May 7, 2026

Y'all, I need help. As you know, I work at Dallas City Hall. I just got moved to the new Volunteer Executioner evaluation group. Now I have to review applications from those assholes all effing day. I can say, 10/10, no doubt, they don't care about "justice." They just wanna kill. You can practically smell their bloodlust through the screen. I've been doing it for a week and I just can't anymore. I tried to talk to my boss about getting out of it but she said there are too many applications and "we all have to help." There are so many applications. It's depressing. So I'm looking for a new job. Any leads for an experienced (7 years) admin assistant send them my way. I've worked in both government and private companies, and I know how to use Office and Mac systems. I need something fast.

Tampa Bay Post, May 13, 2026: Swift and Senate propose amendment to 1HA allowing a second murder – for a price

Governor Mark Swift introduced an amendment to the One Homicide Act that would allow people who have already used their one murder would be permitted to "buy" another one. "This will pump money into our economy and ensure a further drop in the crime rate by eliminating bad people," reads the official statement from the Office of the Governor website. The price of obtaining a second murder will be five thousand dollars. Several state legislators, all Republicans, have voiced support for the amendment.

However, State Senator David Hume, architect of 1HA, promised in a statement on his website to vote against it. "This goes against my intent behind the One Homicide Act. Everybody was supposed to have equal access. Under this amendment, whoever has an extra five thousand dollars lying around can buy their way to a second murder. Most Floridians do not have that kind of money. I honestly don't understand the Governor's reasoning behind this."

Swift claimed in his own press conference that the money from Second Homicide, the proposed title of the amendment, would go to "anti-drug programs and fixing our schools." Despite several requests, Swift's office has yet to release a budget or provide details on how the proposed extra proceeds would be distributed.

It is believed that the Second Homicide amendment was a reaction to the rejection of the "high-value resident" exemption proposed by Sen. Phyllis Taylor late last year, which would have ensured protection against 1HA murders for any residents with an annual income greater than $500,000. The measure was unpopular with the public and did not pass committee. Sen. Taylor could not be reached for comment.

Concord Times, May 16, 2026: Woman sues state for emotional distress after witnessing Correction Act murder

Concord resident Darlene Cook filed a lawsuit against the state of New Hampshire citing "civic negligence" in passing the Correction Act. The controversial law allows each state resident to murder one person without legal consequences. Cook is claiming emotional distress after witnessing a man getting shot in a grocery store parking lot. "I was walking to my car and this man just collapsed in front of me. His head was covered with blood. Then the guy who shot him smiled and walked away, holding his gun." Cook choked back tears. "I swear I heard people clap. Like they were watching a movie. It was disgusting. I still see that poor man when I close my eyes." Cook revealed that she voted against the law "for a lot of reasons. But this, this was far worse than anything I imagined."

The state's attorney cites a precedent from Florida, which ruled that civil action could not be filed in response to murders committed under their "murder law," the One Homicide Act. Cook's attorney countered in a statement: "I am well aware of the Florida court's ruling. However, that only applied to family members of victims filing wrongful death suits against the state. Ms. Cook was an innocent bystander who saw a grisly sight. Her subsequent mental anguish was a foreseeable consequence of the state's actions, and the state needs to be held liable. As long as these 'legal' murders are committed in public, more citizens will be traumatized."

Dr. Sophia Young, a psychologist at the University of New Hampshire, finds validity in Cook's claim. "Witnesses of violent events such as murders can suffer severe psychological symptoms, such as anxiety and panic attacks. It's also common for them to develop PTSD."

Several mental health organizations, including the American Psychological Association, are recommending a limitation on murders committed in public as a protective measure. "Ideally, the One Homicide Act and its imitators wouldn't exist at all," says Dr. Randolph Pearson, vice president of the APA. "But it appears these laws aren't going away. The least governments can do is protect innocent bystanders from having to see horrific acts in public."

The governor's office and State Senator Thomas Loeb, who introduced the Correction Act, did not respond to interview requests.

Tallahassee Daily, May 19, 2026: 1HA architect Hume resigns, dodges questions about Swift allegations

State Senator David Hume sent shockwaves through the state when he announced his resignation this morning. A video statement released on his official website was brief and cryptic: "Due to circumstances beyond my control, I can no longer serve in the Florida state legislature. I hope the public and the press will respect my and my family's privacy during this difficult time." His office says Hume "will not be granting interviews at this time."

In the last few years, Hume became an infamous figure in Florida and nationwide after spearheading the One Homicide Act. Since its passing, the One Homicide Act, or 1HA, has inspired fierce debate and spawned imitators in other states.

Sources close to Hume say he was "disheartened" after several amendments he drafted were voted down by the legislature. "He told me he saw how the law was being used, how Swift and his cronies were using it to push their own agenda. After the abortion protection was shot down again, and then Swift pushed for the high value resident ban, you could see his spirit dying." A source identifying themselves as a former Hume aide echoes this statement: "His efforts kept getting undermined. He was exhausted. I could see it in his face."

These sources also say Hume was "disgusted" with how the One Homicide Act turned out in practice. A former aide said Hume was "shocked" by the statistic that nearly 40 percent of Florida residents filed Intent to Murder applications. "He thought it would be ten, at most 15 percent."

Hume's former colleague Dorothy Ross says the "final straw" for Hume was the Second Homicide amendment. "He told me, this thing was supposed to be equal. But Swift and his cronies are saying that if you pay enough, you can kill more. He said that was in total opposition to his original intent. Even though I still disagree with 1HA, I admire Hume's efforts to make changes to aspects he saw as harmful. But it belongs to Swift now. He's a dangerous man, and he's turned Florida into a dangerous place." Ross left Florida after losing her bid for reelection in 2024 because "I absolutely feared for my life. I didn't have the public figures protection anymore and I know the 1HA devotees are not happy with me. If I stayed, I know it only would have been a matter of time before I got a Target Notice."

Swift did not respond to requests for comment.

YouTube Statement, May 23, 2026: "Murder Law" Content No Longer Permitted

Due to user complaints and our desire to foster an inclusive atmosphere, YouTube will no longer permit videos of live murders committed under "murder laws." We will also be removing any current 1HA-related content. We want this to be a place for enjoyment, not violence.

Bluesky, @northcountrygirl, May 28, 2026

I was invited to visit some college friends in Miami this summer. But with #1HA, no way I'm going to Florida. The constant threat of seeing a murder isn't my idea of a relaxing vacation. US, your neighbors to the north are legit worried about you.

Baton Rouge Press, May 30, 2026: Senator Carrouth proposes dueling law

State Senator Peter Carrouth presented his proposal for the Honor Restoration Act to the Senate floor yesterday. The law will allow Louisiana residents to challenge another resident to a fight, or "trial by combat," if the challenger feels he or she has been wronged by another party.

The senator said in his presentation that the new law will "iron out the imperfections" of the controversial "murder laws" that have been enacted in other states, beginning with Florida's One Homicide Act, which was passed in 2023. "The Honor Restoration Act will not be an open license to kill. Applicants will go through a strict vetting process. They won't just fill out an application to be approved by low-level state employees. The initial applications will be reviewed by specially trained attorneys and county clerks before they go to the next phase. If the initial application is approved, then both the applicant and the intended opponent will be required to present evidence before a judge. The judge will have the final decision on whether or not a duel will take place."

The duels will be open to public spectators for an admission price "to be determined on the local level." This money, Carrouth said, will go toward Louisiana public schools. The Louisiana Teachers Association wrote on X in response: "We do not support this barbaric plan. Tax the one percent and stop wasting taxpayer money on sports arenas. That's the way to get money for schools."

Carrouth says he "has the votes" to get the law through committee and onto November's ballot. "Our current system all too often coddles criminals and overlooks victims. Now victims who have been let down by the courts will have a new avenue to pursue justice."

Poll: Do you support the Honor Restoration Act?

Yes: 51 percent

No: 42 percent

Undecided: 7 percent

Florida Independent, May 29, 2026: Anonymous source reveals details behind Tate's 1HA Murder

Shockwaves were sent through Florida and the country last week when the House Ethics Committee called for an investigation into Rep. Bill Tate, who was revealed to have killed under the One Homicide Act.

Governor Mark Swift released a statement in support of Tate on X (formerly Twitter): "Congressman Tate acted in accordance with the law. Whatever your opinion of the One Homicide Act, the fact is, in the eyes of Florida's legal system, he did nothing wrong. The House Dems are using this as a pretext for a preemptive takedown of his popular policies."

According to public 1HA records, Congressman Tate committed his murder in 2024, just after he announced his campaign. The target was Kevin Brooks, a former employee of Tate's corporate consulting firm Terracotta Consulting. Tate cited "intimidation and harassment" as the reason for wanting to kill Brooks. A police report of Brooks waiting outside Tate's residence and accosting him was included with the application. However, an anonymous source contacted this publication with information suggesting a more sinister motive.

The source, a former Terracotta employee, claims that Brooks "knew too much" about Tate's criminal activities. "He killed Kevin to shut him up. Simple as that. Tate has friends in Sarasota City Hall. He and the deputy mayor went to school together. He could have said anything on his application and one of them would have pushed it through."

When asked what Brooks knew, the source said, "Tate was into underage girls. We all heard the stories. He would hang around high schools. One of his frat buddies was a gym teacher at a prep school outside Sarasota. Kevin called me after he left Terracotta and told me this teacher would literally drive girls to Tate's condo. It was sick. I quit after hearing that. I didn't want to work for a pedophile. I reported it to the police but I don't think anything came of it. It's not like I had any hard proof, just stories. Tate has friends there too. I looked up the school and the teacher is still there. The thing is, Brooks had proof. He said he'd found pictures in Tate's office. I definitely think that's why Tate killed him. He made up some fake motive on his application to cover his ass."

When asked if any of Tate's alleged victims ever came forward, the source said, "I don't know. From what I heard, there were a lot of them. So at least one of them had to say something. But Tate knows a lot of powerful people. He could have paid them off or threatened their families. It wouldn't surprise me."

The source then revealed why he would only speak under the terms of anonymity: "Kevin and I had been secretly investigating this since we left Terracotta. When I heard that Kevin was murdered, I knew it was Tate. I went to Kevin's house after the funeral and looked for his records. They were all gone. I know in my gut that Tate destroyed them. But I had copies of some of Kevin's notes. I sent them to the House Ethics Committee when I heard Tate was running for office."

The source said he has also sent a formal complaint to the state of Florida alleging fraud in Tate's application. Under the One Homicide Act, if the Department of Homicide Assessment finds evidence that Tate fabricated part of his application, the murder will be investigated and prosecuted as an illegal homicide.

The source said he left Florida shortly after leaving Terracotta. "I got a job out of the state, and I wanted to get as far away as possible. If I was still there, I don't know what Tate would do to me. But I know he'd do something."

Representative Tate and Governor Swift did not respond to requests for comment.

Huffington Post, June 1, 2026: I killed under the One Homicide Act. I wish I hadn't.

Everybody is talking about the One Homicide Act. You can't open Twitter (now X, I guess) or Facebook without seeing an opinion about it. Well, I took advantage of it. And I have regretted it ever since.

I applied to kill the pharmacist who gave my daughter the opioids she ODed on. Not the doctor who prescribed them. Not the CEO at the pharma company pushing them on patients and paying off doctors. The pharmacist, who was just doing her job. Her name was the only one I knew and I wanted somebody to pay.

To be honest, I was a little drunk when I filled out the application. If I'd had to wait even one or two more days, I probably would have snapped out of it. But the acceptance came so quick I was still hopped up on rage.

I submitted my application online on a Wednesday night, I got my murder certificate in my email the following Monday. It's so hard to admit now, but I was excited. I killed her the following week with my husband's gun.

It was when I saw her parents coming back from her funeral that I started feeling guilty. They looked so sad. But I told myself she had done a bad thing, and it was my right, so it was okay.

But it wasn't. The bad feeling didn't go away. My husband and I had been having problems ever since our daughter died. He tried to talk me out of the murder. Shortly after I did it, he left me. He said he didn't like who I'd become. We'd been married for almost 30 years.

During the divorce, I started therapy. I've now come to terms with my daughter's death. I got involved with a group that helps addicts in their recovery. Trying to make something good out of this tragedy. It's what I should have done from the start. Now not only is my daughter still dead, so is another innocent woman.

I'm worried that more of the hundreds of people who have killed under 1HA and the other laws will also end up regretting it. Maybe not now, but eventually. I don't care how mad you are, how bad that person hurt you. Killing doesn't feel good. And if you think it does, you need to look at yourself. Talk to a friend, talk to a therapist. Find another way past the anger and grief, one that doesn't involve taking a life and causing more hurt.

TechTalk.com, June 5, 2026: Hughes announces new video sharing platform

Eli Hughes, founder of software company Total Solutions Tech, announced plan to launch a new video sharing platform called FreeVids, in a move that is believed to be a response to YouTube's ban on what it called "murder law content."

Hughes has been an outspoken champion of the controversial laws since Florida's One Homicide Act passed in 2023, penning an op-ed in the New York Times titled "Why Florida (and America) need the One Homicide Act." Records also reveal that he contributed over one million dollars to Florida Governor Mark Swift's 2020 election campaign, shortly after he relocated his company's headquarters from San Jose to Miami.

"There will be no censorship on FreeVids," Hughes said in a statement on his website, reposted on X (formerly Twitter). "Murder laws like 1HA have greatly benefited this country. My new platform will be a free place to share that and all content."

Reddit, which hosts a large volume of One Homicide Act-related content, including people sharing their murder stories and how to "fake citizenship" in sponsoring states, issued a statement in response to the YouTube story: "We trust our admins to properly regulate any inappropriate content. We see no need to issue sweeping condemnations and restrictions." TikTok, where users frequently livestream their legal murders, has no official plans to ban such content.

FreeVids is advertised to go live on July 4.

One Stop News Source, June 13, 2026: Further allegations emerge against Florida Governor

A former Florida court clerk who reviewed One Homicide Act applications contacted this reporter with further allegations against Governor Mark Swift. They only agreed to speak under the condition of anonymity.

"I wasn't sure what to make of it at first," the source said. "But then I started thinking. Like, I remember seeing a lot of applications for people I'd heard about in the news. Not like famous people or anything. But I found some of the first applications and looked up the names, and a lot of them were mentioned in stories about Swift. Like they had beef with him, things like that. Then I believed it."

State Senator Brad Canale was the only Florida lawmaker who responded to our requests for comment. He wrote in an email, "This is exactly why I oppose 1HA. It's Waterson all over again.

The rich and powerful have always exploited the law for their own purposes. And this is literally life and death they're toying with for their own selfish motives."

Governor Swift's office did not respond to requests for comment.

Reddit, r/NewHampshire, June 18, 2026: Don't use Hood Contractors, they're anti-Correction Act and anti-freedom

I quit my job at Hood today to protest their new anti-freedom policy. Last week they made an announcement saying any employee who killed under the Correction Act would be fired. Y'all know the state motto, Live Free or Die, right? Hood Contractors seems to think it's Live Free and Get Fired. They said our customers might be "uncomfortable" if they had a contractor who killed somebody and a lot of them do background checks on us. When I quit, I said, "Maybe don't tell them. Why do they have a right to know what we do in our personal lives?" Apparently everybody who takes advantage of the Correction Act goes on a public record, also bullshit. Whatever happened to privacy?

Anyway, fuck Hood Contractors. They're firing law-abiding citizens. The Correction Act is the law whether you like it or not. Just cause they wanna court big clients in liberal hellhole Boston we have to suffer. Cause this is what it's all about. Don't believe their ass-covering lies.

A bunch of us have quit. We're looking into suing them for discrimination. If anybody knows a good lawyer in the Manchester area or wants to donate to our GoFundMe, DM me.

Blue Flags: A Liberal Voice for Change, June 21, 2026: Casting a light on the extremist libertarian cabal behind America's murder laws

Three US states, Florida, Arizona, and New Hampshire, now have "murder laws", meaning everybody can kill one person in their life, as long as they have an approved application and follow the rules. Several other states, including Alabama, Nevada, Utah, and Louisiana, have similar laws in the works.

The state officials behind the laws claimed they had studies to back up their claims of decreased crime and flourishing economies, but a deep dive behind the scenes reveals something less official that screams special interest pandering.

Who's behind the murder laws? A far-right radical libertarian group that proudly proclaims themselves above the law. "Human nature is not criminal. Society's laws deem human nature criminal" is the quote in the banner heading on their website and social media pages. And, in a not at all surprising revelation, has a massive following in murder law states.

The Stirner Society were said to be the driving force behind Florida's One Homicide Act, the law that started it all. David Hume, the state senator who drafted the law, was once a member but disavowed the group when pressed by a reporter during his first run for the senate. "I still support the Stirner Society's philosophy of individual freedom and personal responsibility. I left because I disagreed with some of their official positions. For instance, I am a firm supporter of a woman's right to reproductive choice, and the Stirner Society is not." Hume also publicly opposed the group's anti-vaccination stance during the pandemic after a member was caught with a homemade bomb outside a vaccine clinic in Tampa. "Vaccines are a marvel of medical science. To oppose them in this day and age is simply foolish," he wrote on his official X (formerly Twitter) account after the incident. Financial records show that Hume stopped paying dues to the Stirner Society in 2010, before he entered politics.

Florida Governor Mark Swift, though never an official member, has received regular donations from the Florida chapter's president, real estate developer Gavin Dalton. Dalton and the Florida chapter publicly supported the One Homicide Act.

A close look at any murder law state will find a strong presence of the Stirner Society. New Hampshire, which passed the Correction Act in 2024, is the site of the group's annual "live off the land" gathering and their state chapter has approximately five thousand members. Texas, home of the Volunteer Executioner Act, is also home to a chapter of over seven thousand, making it the second largest chapter in the country. The largest is in Arizona, with approximately eight thousand members. Arizona is also home to the Individual Justice Act, which has the dubious distinction of being the murder law with the least restrictions, according to a report by Politico.

The Stirner Society of Louisiana, with around two thousand members, has lobbied heavily for that state's Honor Restoration Act, set to go to the polls this November. "One individual against another, and the strongest, the best, survives. That's how every conflict should be resolved. One to one. No laws, no social codes," the Louisiana chapter wrote on its official Facebook page. Utah, where the Atonement Act will be on the ballot in the next election, has a chapter with almost four thousand members, including former Attorney General Nathan Farr.

The Stirner Society is not a peaceful group. It has been linked to terrorist attacks across the country. In 2021, a member in Phoenix set a vaccine clinic on fire. The member posted on the Arizona chapter's official TikTok page, unidentified with a face in shadow: "No mandatory untested medical procedures. We will not be the government's guinea pigs." The perpetrator was later identified as twenty-six-year-old Andrew Kennedy, an unemployed Phoenix resident. He is currently serving a ten-year sentence for arson.

Tech billionaire Eli Hughes, a vocal supporter of murder laws, also has ties to the Stirner Society, though there is no record of him ever being an official member. The vice president of the Nevada chapter, casino magnate John Miller, provided Hughes' company with startup money. Hughes has also praised the group online and donated to chapters in Florida, Nevada, and California.

FreeVids, July 4, 2026: A message from Eli Hughes

Welcome to Free Vids. While every other corner of the internet is bowing to the woke mob and the sissyfication of the country, we stand for free speech. All speech. I was targeted by a murder application in Florida. I was in Miami setting up a new branch of my company. And some hippie commie who hates free enterprise because he's a failure tried to kill me. But you know what, I defended myself. I pushed the knife out of his hand and my bodyguard tackled him. All these "victims" whining, oh I almost died. Or that crybaby who tried to sue after his wife died. You know you have the right to defend yourselves, right? It's written into the law. Your friends or whoever who got killed, they just weren't trying hard enough to stay alive. If you're about to die, you fight. If you don't fight, I know it's not PC or woke or whatever, but maybe they deserved to die. They knew what was coming, that's part of the law. But they died anyway. Because they were weak. That's what's wrong with this country. Too many crybabies blaming the "government" or white men to avoid taking taking personal responsibility. And the Second Homicide that the left is whining about, guess what, that's how America works. We job creators who actually work for a living get more than those of you begging for handouts. Again, not PC don't care. The One Homicide Act is helping weed out the weak. That's why FreeVids will not censor 1HA content, or any content. This is a 100 percent free speech zone. No restrictions, no PC police, no woke mob. FreeVids represents what America should be: free speech for all.

Tallahassee Times, July 5, 2026: Hume Book Announced

One year after State Senator David Hume's abrupt resignation, bestselling author and former Miami Herald political correspondent Samuel Wells announced on his official website and on Twitter that he was co-writing Hume's memoir, set to be published by Random House "in the coming year." Wells did not go into detail, but promised "powerful revelations about Hume's time in office."

TikTok, @panhandlegirl81: Swift is shady AF #1HA

I worked at the State House. I heard all the stories. Everyone there says Governor Swift has killed a bunch of people under 1HA. There's no way to prove it. All the evidence is circumstantial. But I know people who killed for him. Some of them are proud they were chosen. Swift's name isn't on any of the applications. He didn't just use staffers. He had staffers recruit other people so nothing could be traced to him. He paid them all off too. He's killing off his enemies and he won't face any consequences. And from what I've heard he's got a lot of enemies.

Even before 1HA, there were stories about Swift. When he first ran for mayor in Naples, a reporter who wrote a negative story suddenly died in a car crash. Nobody had any proof, but everybody just knew in their gut that Swift had something to do with it. Anybody else who was maybe gonna speak out against him saw what happened and kept quiet. Just like everybody at the State House is keeping quiet now.

Tallahassee Daily, July 22, 2026: Former State Senator Hume Found Dead, Killer Acted Under 1HA

David Hume, former Florida State Senator and architect of the controversial One Homicide Act, from was found dead this morning of a gunshot wound to the head outside his Orlando home. Hume was named as a victim on an Intent to Murder application, which was approved. The killer avoided the "no public figures" clause by the fact that Hume was no longer in office. The stated reason for the murder was not released, given the latest provisions to 1HA signed by Governor Swift.

The medical examiner said Hume's body showed "no signs of struggle." Hume's wife and teenage daughter were at the family's vacation house in Key West at the time of the murder.

Miami Herald, July 27, 2026: Writer of Hume Biography Survives 1HA Attempt

Former Herald reporter and best-selling author Samuel Wells was attacked by an intruder in his Miami Beach home while he slept. He did not sustain any serious injuries. The assailant has not yet been identified.

Wells posted a statement on his website and on Twitter, where he revealed that he was named as a target on three Intent to Murder applications. His assailant has not yet been identified. "I don't want to rehash all the details just yet. I'm still shaken by the whole thing."

Wells believes the attack is related to his work on a book with late State Senator David Hume, who was killed last month under the One Homicide Act. "I don't think it's a coincidence that I got targeted right after announcing I would be publishing the Hume interview transcripts. I don't know which of the three people who applied to kill me attacked me. It was dark, I didn't see his face. I fought him off and he ran out of my room."

Wells, a Miami Beach native, said that he has permanently left the state to avoid any further attempts on his life. "As a born and bred Floridian, this is hard to say, but I doubt I will be returning anytime soon," he said in his online statement.

Due to allegations around Governor Mark Swift related to the One Homicide Act, rumors have circulated that Hume's murder and the attack on Wells were orchestrated by Swift to silence Hume after news broke that Hume would be publishing a memoir. Governor Swift has not responded to these allegations or made any public comments about the attacks on Hume and Wells.

GoFundMe: Help me get my second murder

I got fucked over by my supposed best friend after he fucked my girlfriend. I applied to kill her right after the law passed. I stabbed her in her bed it was fuckin awesome. Bitch got what was coming to her. But my ex friend is saying all this shit like she didn't deserve it. And I realized he needs to die too. He knew she was my girlfriend and he fucked her anyway. Now we can get a second murder. And I need it to get closure on the worst thing that ever happened to me. But I can't afford it. You need $100 to even file the application, then $2000 to get your murder if its approved. I'm doing this for every guy who ever got their heart broken by a lying cheating bitch and a weak fake friend. I promise to take video and send it to everyone who donates. I'll send a pic of my bitch ex's bloody body to the top three donors.

Facebook, Nina Sayles, July 30, 2026

I've lived in New Hampshire most of my adult life, and for the first time I'm thinking about leaving, because of the Correction Act. I get scared whenever I walk down the street. I'm afraid I'll hear a gunshot or see a body drop on the sidewalk. I used to love walking in the park near my house. But it was the scene of a murder last week. Now I can't go there. I'm afraid I'll see someone getting killed. I believe in freedom as much as the next person, but there's gotta be a limit.

FreeVids, Gen X Goldwater, August 4, 2026: I killed David Hume

It was me. I killed that traitor Hume. Here's my approved application and my completion notice. With a photo of the body. Fuck Hume. He was bending over for the libs and trying to destroy his own creation. And fuck everybody saying I was coerced by Governor Swift. Swift didn't tell me to do it, but I did it for him. He's getting dragged through the mud and I knew that sellout Hume would just make things worse. He was gonna tell a bunch of lies to cover his own ass. Don't ask me how I know I just do. The bastard needed to go. I did it for all freedom-loving Floridians. Keep Florida and America free.

Facebook, Duncan Powell, August 5, 2026

This douchebag bragging on right-wing YouTube is Roy Graham. I went to high school with him. He's a fucking loser, always was, always will be. He bullied everybody in school, including me, but he still lives on the same block in Panama City. He's 48 and still works in a parking garage. Now he's trying to be some kind of badass. Fuck that guy and fuck 1HA.

FreeVids, @GodGunsAndTexas: I'm an official executioner

Hey y'all, check this out. Yeah, my execution application got approved. Yeah, it's bullshit that I don't get to pick the prisoner. It's assigned by lottery or some shit. I won't find out who I got until next year, it says. Long time to wait, but it'll be worth it. Ya boy is gonna be taking action and cleaning up the scum. I'll let y'all know how it goes. I'd bring you in with me if I could, but no cameras allowed. Fuck that. We should broadcast executions. Let the criminals know what's coming to them if they don't wanna live by our laws.

Samuel Wells Official Website, August 16, 2026: Hume Memoir Materials Available Today

I was working with former Florida State Senator David Hume on his memoir at the time of his tragic death. Mr. Hume contacted me shortly after his resignation, saying he had "a story that needed to be told." With the permission of Mr. Hume's family, I am publishing all interview transcripts and notes on my site. Access is free, but donations are welcome. Per Mrs. Hume's request, all proceeds will go to 1HA Survivors, a charity benefiting the families of people killed as a result of the One Homicide Act, and End Legal Murder, a grassroots political organization devoted to stopping similar laws.

David Hume Interview Transcript

W: What brought about the One Homicide Act?

H: Um, I guess, it wasn't as scientific as I made it out to be. I'd read studies about rehabilitation of criminals through allowing "small offenses," and some psychological case studies about the murderous impulses inside all of us, and just extrapolated. There are these stories about people acting outside the law and solving their own problems. People who subdued intruders, found blackmailers, foiled potential mass shooters. I read about Ken McElroy in Missouri. He terrorized an entire town but, due to red tape and loopholes in an unjust system, he kept avoiding consequences for his actions. Then the people of the town joined forces and killed him. None of them would talk to the police, so nobody was arrested. But they were free from this bully. I was inspired by those stories. I thought, maybe, somebody who couldn't go through the normal legal channels needed an alternative to get justice. That was what I thought the One Homicide Act would be. But it didn't turn out like that. I - I just thought people would be more responsible with it.

W: What do you mean?

H: I only thought a few people would apply. And that the ones who did would have good reasons. I never thought there would be so many. And I never ever thought they would do it for such petty reasons. Maybe I was naïve. Too hopeful. But I thought, I thought it would maybe be used for good, like a woman freeing herself from an abusive partner, you know, something like that. I guess I have too much faith in people. [*Long pause while Hume shook his head*] 1HA is the biggest regret of my career. No, my life.

W: Do you have anything to say about the allegations against Governor Mark Swift?

H: Yes. Based on what I know they're all true.

W: What do you know?

H: I know he filed an Intent to Murder application. One of my staffers showed it to me after it was approved.

W: Who did Governor Swift kill?

H: I am not comfortable divulging that information at the moment.

W: Did you ever commit a murder under the One Homicide Act?

H: No. I never even considered it. I thought that made me an example. If the person who created the law didn't take advantage of it, then not many people will. But a friend of mine did. That was the first inkling I had that maybe it wasn't as good an idea as I thought.

W: How so?

H: He called me after his murder to tell me about it. He thanked me, saying, I'll never forget it, "Thank you for giving me the right to do things the way they should be done." The way he said it was just off-putting in a way I couldn't articulate. He just seemed way too happy. I intended the One Homicide Act as a last resort for people who slipped through the cracks of the justice system, something they had to do to get piece of mind. But my friend, former friend, he took such pleasure in it. After that, I couldn't be around him anymore. But I still supported the law. I still believed it would be good for the state, for the country. I still thought there were people out there that would benefit from it. I knew it needed work, and I thought I could make it work. But that uneasy feeling I had around my former friend was still there, making me question whether I was doing the right thing. I tried to ignore it, push it out of my head. I felt like I couldn't go back on 1HA, no matter how bad I felt. Then I heard more stories. I saw the videos. And I just hit a breaking point. I couldn't support it anymore.

W: What was that breaking point?

H: I saw one video online. And it was enough. I couldn't serve in a legislature that continued to support that law and block my efforts to change it. Before I only thought about the law in abstract terms. I was told from the second I entered politics to only look at numbers. "Facts." [*Hume used air quotes over that word in the interview.*] I never considered the human costs. But I saw a video of a bullet hitting a woman in the head. She just dropped, right at her front door. The killer was her ex-boyfriend. He was laughing the whole time. I later learned she was supposed to have dinner with her mother that evening. The mother was frantic with worry. Then she had to get that terrible news. I thought about, about, if it was one of my kids. [*Hume started crying here.*] I realized then just what I had done. The next morning, I requested an emergency meeting with Governor Swift. I told him we needed to repeal 1HA. It was doing far more harm than good. I even showed him the video. I had to look away, but he watched the whole thing and his expression didn't change. He just said, and I'll never forget it, "Crime is down. That's all that matters." And he was real happy that tourism was up. Because people were hoping to see murders in the streets. It's sick. Fuck it. [*Note: It was odd hearing Hume swear. Despite the high levels of emotion, he was composed throughout most of our interview. But his composure broke here.*] I'll tell you who Swift killed. It was his ex-wife. His first ex-wife, the one he thought we didn't know about. They got married after he knocked her up in high school. Then he left her. They officially got married and divorced in Georgia, so no Florida documents. The story was, and I heard this from his former assistant, so I have no reason to doubt it, she threatened to go to the press unless he paid her off. And he did, for years. But then she wanted more. So he killed her. I'm sure he lied on the application, or had a staffer push it through. I looked at it and, under the guidelines, it shouldn't have been approved. His ex-wife lived in Georgia. She hadn't lived in Florida for years. And she was killed in Georgia. I tried to talk to the head of the Department of Homicide Assessment, but he wouldn't do anything about it. He just said, "Swift had a valid reason. This woman was a very real danger to him." Even if that was true, she lived outside the state. He had no right to kill her.

W: Why are you revealing all of this now?

H: Because I have to. I told my wife, I have to do this. She wanted me to go into protective custody, but I refused. I am taking full responsibility for my hand in starting this mess. I don't want to be protected, not after I let so many people down.

Reddit, r/Louisiana, August 21, 2026: I got a first look at the dueling law and it is wild

Using a throwaway so it can't be traced to me. I'm about to spill some serious super-secret tea. No NDA or anything, but I feel better staying anonymous. I work for a state senator (no, not saying which one), and I've seen the first drafts of the Honor Restoration Act, the dueling law. There's some messed up shit in there even for our backward ass state.

In a lot of ways it looks better than Florida's murder law. But being slightly less fucked up than Florida isn't exactly a flex. Senator Carrouth said there'd be rules. And there are. A lot of them. But they're fucking wild.

Here's what you gotta do if you wanna duel: gather evidence against whoever you wanna duel, like police reports, threatening texts, security cam video. Then you write up a petition. I don't know exactly what it would look like but I think it's just a summary of the evidence and why you think you should be allowed to fight this person to the death. Then you give the petition to the court, I think you can submit it online but I'm not 100% on that, then you either get a rejection notice or a court summons to appear before a judge so they can rule on whether the duel can happen. Oh, the person you wanna duel also gets a notice because they have to go too and they can give a counter argument. The judge hears from both people involved and makes a decision either for or against the duel. If it's approved both parties have to prepare for the next hearing: determining the terms of the duel.

I don't know how that part works, I think they're is still working on that part.

That's all I know so far. Happy to answer any questions I can and will provide updates.

Edit: Somebody asked if the other person can refuse to duel, and I honestly don't know.

FloridaNews.net, August 26, 2026: Swift dodges questions about Hume revelations

At yesterday's press conference, Governor Mark Swift notably dodged several questions about revelations from late State Senator David Hume, published online by journalist Samuel Wells yesterday. He even tossed out a Miami Herald reporter for repeatedly asking, "Any comments on the Hume story?"

Instead, Swift discussed the dropping crime rates and continued to tout tourism revenue. However, those claims have been repeatedly disputed. Florida tourism has decreased sharply since the beginning of 2026, with many on social media specifically citing the One Homicide Act and the current political climate as reasons for staying away. The dropping crime rates, according to a Florida State University statistician, are "subject to dispute." Details are in the links below.

TikTok, @eattherich, August 29, 2026: Rot in piss Hume #End1HA

Hot take: Hume deserved to get killed. Some y'all mighta been fooled by his bullshit notpology but it didn't fool me. It was still all his fault in the first place. He coulda introduced a new bill. He coulda released his "evidence." Why didn't he speak up before? Waiting until he was out of office to profit off a fucking book. Coward move. He deserved to die. Not just for that, for everything he did. Cutting taxes on the autocrats, cutting restrictions and letting big business get even bigger. Truth bomb: he was a shitty person. Stop letting shitty white men apologize their way out of accepting consequences. Rot in hell Hume.

TikTok, @samuelwellswriter, August 30, 2026: Response to @eattherich David Hume was a good man and I miss him

That video was the most disgusting thing I've seen on TikTok. And that's saying a lot. I spent over two weeks with David Hume. He was genuinely remorseful about the One Homicide Act. He cried several times during our interviews. He saw the error of his actions. And he "spoke up" numerous times. He introduced one amendment after another and they never passed. That was not his fault. His family is heartbroken right now. Random strangers hiding behind their devices saying he deserved to die, without knowing him, is everything that's wrong with this platform. I know you think you're being edgy or progressive or "brutally honest" or whatever self-congratulatory shield you've erected for yourselves. Let David's murder remind us what's wrong with 1HA. It relies on brute force and a simplified solution to complex problems. David tore himself apart over 1HA until the day he died. Remember that there are human beings receiving your insults.

World News Desk, United States News, August 31, 2026: US-style "murder laws" spreading around the world

In 2023, Florida passed the One Homicide Act, which permits each resident one "free murder": they can apply to kill someone and if it's approved, they can kill that person with no legal consequences. Other states in the US soon followed suit. Despite numerous controversies, such as allegations of fraud and bias in the review of the applications, the laws remain popular. Several other states have similar laws on the ballot in November's elections, and are starting to spread around the globe.

A spokesperson for the President of the Philippines announced the recently enacted Personal Justice Code at a press conference in Manila last week. "So many of our citizens have been wronged by the criminal element infesting our nation. These people cannot be reformed. They need to be eliminated. What better way to achieve that than to let their victims take action? What's one less thieving junkie, one less cheating wife? If you don't do bad things you have nothing to worry about."

Hungary is planning similar legislation, with the press minister specifically touting the "success" of the One Homicide Act in an email to this publication: "Law abiding Hungarians have been terrorized by murderous thieving gangs for too long. America's One Homicide Act is giving power back to the people and permanently removing criminals from society. Hungarians deserve the right to fight back against the oppressive criminal element that has invaded our country." No official plan for a murder law has been released by the Hungarian Parliament.

Turkey is also rumored to have a murder law in the works. However, Turkish officials did not respond to requests for confirmation.

Reddit, "Floridians Against 1HA": I work at the State House, here's what went down with the David Hume murder

Posted this in 1HA Stories but got downvoted and harassed by the pro 1HA nuts so I took it down. The day after Hume resigned at least five applications to kill him came in. I rejected one because it didn't have a Social Security number or an address. That week we got a bunch more. Dozens. A lot of people wanted to kill him. One called him a traitor. I approved one but it wasn't the guy who ended up killing him. After he died the office got a bunch of calls and emails complaining that they didn't get to kill him. One even threatened to sue. Said killing Hume was his right and we shouldn't have approved more than one application to kill him.

New Hampshire Free Press, October 11, 2026: Activist group calls for repeal of Correction Act

A Manchester-based group called Correct the Correction Act held a protest outside the State House today, accompanied by over four hundred supporters, calling for a repeal of the controversial "murder law."

In an interview after the demonstration, group leader Marcia Rowland cited the death of former Florida State Senator David Hume, the architect of the One Homicide Act, the country's first murder law, and the "disturbing" allegations against Florida Governor Mark Swift, as well as personal stories of trauma, as reasons for the protest.

"It's making all of us more tense," she said. "I've gotten to the point where I'm afraid to open my email. Who knows who might have some kind of petty grievance against me and try to kill me? People get mad over the stupidest things. And now they can take it to the extreme."

A recent poll suggested that, in just three months since the passing of the Correction Act, support has dropped by almost ten percent. Polls from other states with murder laws note similar trends. In Florida, approval of the One Homicide Act is down by nineteen percent, and Governor Swift's approval rating dropped twelve percent after allegations that he abused the law for personal gain. Arizona's Individual Justice Act, while holding steady in the polls, has been the subject of allegations of fraud and mismanagement.

A spokesperson for New Hampshire Governor Neil Barrett wrote in an email to this reporter: "There are no plans to repeal the Correction Act. We just got the crime statistics in yesterday. Since the passing of the law violent crime is down 38 percent. The measure is a success. We respect the concerns of our citizens, but their views are not in line with the electorate at large, who, according to polls, support the law."

Washington Post, October 22, 2026: Families of murder law victims file class action suit against Hughes website

Over two hundred family members of people killed under state murder laws have filed a class action suit against Eli Hughes' video sharing site FreeVids, citing emotional distress. The group's attorney claims the Supreme Court decision prohibiting One Homicide Act lawsuits in Florida does not apply to this case: "That decision clearly states that victims and their families cannot file suit against the murderers themselves. This is different. FreeVids is profiting from the pain and suffering of countless people and they need to be held accountable."

Hughes did not respond to requests for comment for this article, but said of the suit in a post on X: "You can bet I'll fight this [expletive]. FreeVids will always be a beacon for free speech."

Politics Daily, November 4, 2026: More States Pass "Murder Laws"

Despite mounting criticisms and allegations of abuse for current "murder laws," as well as revelations about late Florida State Senator David Hume's regrets in drafting the One Homicide Act, yesterday's elections saw the passage of similar laws in four states: Oklahoma, Alabama, Nevada, and Pennsylvania. New Jersey's Retribution Act was defeated with 64 percent of the vote.

Louisiana narrowly passed the Honor Restoration Act, which gives residents the right to request a duel to the death with another party. This measure, says Louisiana State Senator Peter Carrouth, who drafted the law, will have "stronger safeguards" than the One Homicide Act. Applicants will have to present evidence before a judge, who will decide if a duel is to be granted.

Volunteer executioner acts, which allow citizens to execute criminals on death row, passed in Tennessee and Nebraska, while a similar proposal in Montana was defeated by 52 percent. The votes on West Virginia's Citizen Vigilance Act and Utah's Atonement Act are still too close to call.

Salt Lake City Tribune, November 9, 2026: Atonement Act officially defeated in recount

The Atonement Act, a "murder law" proposed by State Senator Boyd Jeffries, was officially pronounced defeated yesterday after a second recount, by a margin of fifty-three percent.

Two state senators who initially backed the measure withdrew their support after the Church State Separation Alliance (CSSA) threatened a lawsuit against the state if it passed, on the grounds that the measure was "heavily influenced" by Mormon doctrine, a charge Jeffries denied. "The Atonement Act is not allied with any creed," he said in a statement after the CSSA announcement. "It's about the individual rights that the citizens of Utah and this nation have demanded and deserve."

The council of the Church of Latter Day Saints also came out against the law, saying it was "not representative of our church and our faith in the current era." However, some factions of the church has voiced support.

Senator Jeffries pledged on his X (formerly Twitter) account to reintroduce the law in a future session. "I believe a majority of Utah residents support the Atonement Act, and, after retooling, it will pass."

Louisiana State Bar Association, Official Website, November 18, 2026: A primer on the Honor Restoration Act

The LSBA has obtained an advance draft of RS 1615, the Honor Restoration Act. Please be advised that the terms and language might change between now and March 1, 2027, when the law officially goes into effect.

The Honor Restoration Act, known colloquially as "the dueling law," has a more intensive application process than similar laws in

Florida or Arizona. As of the current date, the procedure is as follows:

1. The applicant, known as the "Challenger," must complete a formal Notice of Challenge and submit it to their local government office. The Notice will consist of the names of the Challenger and their intended opponent, referred to as the "Opponent," and the Challenger's reasons for requesting a duel. The Notice must be accompanied by at least one piece of evidence, such as a police report or record of misconduct on the part of the Opponent. The Notice must include a wet ink signature and a notary stamp.

2. If the Notice is approved by the State, the Opponent receives a Notice of Duel Request with a copy of the Notice of Challenge. The Opponent has thirty days to submit a Notice of Appeal of Duel Request, with any counterarguments to the Challenger's initial arguments. Alternatively, the Opponent can waive the right to appeal, in which case they can sign a Formal Waiver of Appeal. The Appeal and the Waiver must be signed in wet ink and notarized.

3. After both the Challenger and the Opponent have submitted their documents, they are reviewed by a judge, who then schedules a hearing for both parties and to determine whether a duel will take place. Both parties are encouraged to have legal counsel for the hearing.

4. Either party can appeal the judge's decision by filing a Notice to Appeal Duel Ruling. If this happens, the judge will review and either deny the appeal or schedule a second hearing. If the appeal is denied, the ruling cannot be appealed again.

5. If the judge decides to permit the duel, the parties and their counsel meet with an arbitrator to agree on the terms.

Many firms across the state have announced plans to form new departments to advise clients on dueling procedure, and that they will need to hire at least one hundred new associates as well as legal assistants. Depending on the volume of clients and unforeseen complexities that could arise from the law's implementation, these firms will likely have to hire even more personnel. State legal counsel and court clerks will also be in demand in anticipation of rising caseloads.

The Honor Restoration Act is complex and will likely be amended before and after March 1. The LSBA will host seminars on the law and procedures beginning in January. See our Events page for details.

Down Under Lowdown, December 6, 2026: Queensland pushing for US-style "murder law"

Australia's long slide into becoming America continues. Now an MP in Queensland (where else?) thinks we should have murder laws like they do over there. It started in Florida, America's Queensland. The senator there who created the first murder law later said he regretted it, but they kept going. Seriously, check out this interview he gave right before he got killed under the law. I guess no politicians bothered reading it.

Anyway, the Queensland MP is proposing a law that has the same principle as America's murder laws. If somebody wrongs you (no details on what qualifies as being "wronged"), you can fill out an application and if it's approved, you can try to kill them. It's pretty much exactly like the one in Florida. Another reason not to go to Queensland. We can only hope other MPs in this moving steadily backward country don't get ideas. Don't let Australia become America.

National News Weekly, December 18, 2026: Governor Swift announces 2028 Presidential bid

After weeks of speculation, Governor Mark Swift announced yesterday that he will officially enter the Republican presidential primary race.

"I will turn the country around like I did with the great state of Florida," Swift said in front of a crowd estimated at around two thousand gathered outside the Florida State House in Tallahassee.

Gov. Swift has been a national figure since 2023, when Florida passed the One Homicide Act. The law, which allows each state resident to commit one murder after receiving approval of an application, has drawn both praise and criticism. Swift addressed the controversial law during his speech: "All innovations throughout history have been met with resistance. I think Florida's falling crime rates, rising budget surplus, and imitators across the country and all over the world speak for themselves. As President, I will fight for a national One Homicide Act."

Swift did not mention the creator of the One Homicide Act, the late Senator David Hume, whose allegations against the governor created a firestorm earlier this year, and who was killed by an assailant acting under the law. Rumors of disagreements between Hume and Swift over the One Homicide Act were said to be behind Hume's sudden resignation from the State Senate shortly before his death.

Swift has been the subject of numerous other allegations related to the One Homicide Act. Two court cases were recently dismissed in Florida courts. However, Carl Bailey, a former assistant attorney general in Naples, where Swift served as mayor from 2016 to 2020, has pledged to continue his investigation into fraud charges related to Swift's 1HA murder, an allegation confirmed by Hume.

Nina Herrera-Jones, a Miami attorney representing a class action suit alleging misconduct by Swift and his appointed head of the Department of Homicide Assessment, said after the case was dismissed in Miami-Dade County Circuit Court, "Even in the absence of laws, Swift has declared himself above the law. We need to show him that he isn't." When reached for comment after Swift's announcement, Herrera-Jones wrote in an email, "Based on what I've learned, Mark Swift should not be President. He is a corrupt and dangerous man."

Several special interest advocacy groups have issued warnings about Swift since rumors of his presidential run began. The Freedom of Identity Coalition released a statement on Bluesky last week: "America's LGBTQIA community is very concerned about the possibility of a Mark Swift presidency. He said that hate crime laws are 'unnecessary.' He supported measures to prevent transgender teenagers from receiving gender affirming care. He refused to address the problem of queer citizens, especially transgender women, being disproportionately targeted under 1HA. If Swift runs, he must be stopped."

Republicans around the country expressed near unanimous support for Swift. Besides the One Homicide Act, other reasons for his popularity in the party include signing the "Heartbeat Bill," which bans abortion after the sixth week of pregnancy, and "cutting bureaucratic fat," to quote Alabama Representative Wallace Jones. Jones, one of Swift's most ardent supporters, said in a TV appearance after Alabama's Self-Protection act passed the state election last month, "The One Homicide Act really freed up funds for police to concentrate on real crimes rather than solving petty disputes. Without state meddling, we can cut taxes and run leaner and meaner. Swift showed us the way. He should be President."

The Florida governor has also made a name for himself abroad. Swift shared on his official website and social media accounts that he received an invitation to meet with the president of the Philippines, which passed its version of a "murder law" earlier this year. Similar laws have also been proposed in Turkey, Hungary, and parts of Australia, though they have yet to make it to the polls. Democratic Maryland Senator Christina Vanderland, an outspoken opponent of murder laws, wrote in an email to this reporter that a Swift presidency would "open the door to the lunatic fringes not only in other states, but all over the world."

Swift praised the international support for murder laws in his speech. "It's clear that the current methods of law enforcement, that leave important decisions in the hands of ivory tower elites who let criminals walk free and disempower the people, are failing. The success of the One Homicide Act is spawning imitators all over the world. Under my leadership, Florida blazed a trail for innovation in government. As President, I will continue this work and fight for an individualist approach to the crime problem. America will once again serve as an inspiration to the rest of the world."